BABE
PIG IN THE CITY

Adapted by Justine Korman and Ron Fontes

Based on the motion picture screenplay written by
George Miller   Judy Morris   Mark Lamprell

Based on characters created by Dick King-Smith

Random House ⌂ New York

www.randomhouse.com/kids

Library of Congress Cataloging-in-Publication Data:
Korman, Justine.
Babe: pig in the city / adapted by Justine Korman and Ron Fontes.
p. cm.
Sequel to: Babe, by Dick King-Smith.
Summary: On a mission to the Big City to save his farm, Babe the pig gets
separated from his Human, the Boss's Wife, and finds himself among
unscrupulous thieves and homeless animals.
ISBN 0-679-89156-0 (trade) — ISBN 0-679-99156-5 (lib. bdg.)
[1. Pigs—Fiction. 2. City and town life—Fiction. 3. Animals—Fiction.]
I. Fontes, Ron. II. King-Smith, Dick. III. Title.
PZ7.K83692Baad 1998 98-23605
[Fic]—dc21

RL: 5.0
Printed in the United States of America 10 9 8 7 6 5 4 3 2 1

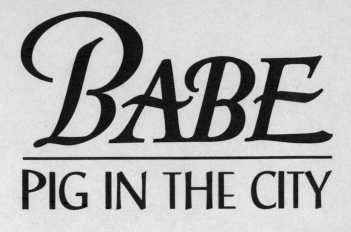

BABE
PIG IN THE CITY

Prologue

Remember, dear ones, the polite little pig who grew up to be a shepherd and a farmer's best friend?

That's right—Babe!

If you promise not to get your fingerprints on it, you may look at the huge brass trophy the two friends won together. The writing says:

NATIONAL SHEEPDOG TRIALS
GRAND CHAMPION
"PIG"
OWNER, A. H. HOGGETT

Indeed, there's nothing true friendship cannot overcome, as you will soon see in this, the story of what happened when Babe and Farmer Hoggett returned to Hoggett Hollow.

Chapter One

If Only

The first hazard for a returning hero is fame. Those who once dismissed you as a lousy pork chop now clamor just to be in your presence. The adulation can spin you quite giddy!

And so it was with Babe.

Babe sat in the back of a jalopy beside his human, Arthur Hoggett. Across his chest, Babe wore a shiny champion's sash. His eyes twinkled as towns-folk waved hats, handkerchiefs, and bright balloons. Fluffy white thistle seeds floated through the air like a gentle ticker-tape parade. Babe could hardly believe all this fuss was for him and his human. All the people were cheering—and the animals, too!

A small boy clutched his bulging jacket as he ran alongside the jalopy. Babe looked down and saw three piglets snuggled in the boy's arms.

"Babe! Babe! Babe!" the piglets squealed.

A horse just beyond the fence whinnied, "You've done us proud, pig!"

Babe lifted his pink snout a bit higher.

Sheep trotted down from the grassy hilltops like woolly white clouds. "Baaaabe! Baaaabe! Ba-a-a-be!" they bleated.

The little pig was starting to feel very big!

Up above, a plane completed a heart around the word PIG. The fluffy letters floated in the blue sky. By the time they reached Hoggett Farm, the small pig was quite swollen with pride.

The farmer's wife came out to meet them as they approached the cottage. Babbling an endless stream of endearments, she folded the farmer in her plump arms.

Meanwhile, the small pig blinked in the glare of flashbulbs. Photographers swarmed around the jalopy like lightning bugs. Babe was a star!

The deeds of the farmer and his remarkable pig had become known even in distant lands. Invitations were coming from all over: To open fairs, to demonstrate sheepherding, even to meet the Queen! But Arthur Hoggett was a quiet man. For him, the best pleasures were to be found in honest work.

So a few days later, Hoggett was glad to be back to business, replacing the old water pump. He hauled the new pump to the edge of the cobblestone well. He placed the heavy pump on a wooden platform, then climbed down into the well. From there he could lower the platform down to the bottom using a rope and pulley. This was the sort of thing the farmer liked to do much more than shaking hands with strangers and smiling for cameras.

Babe, still intoxicated with his fame, got it into his head that he could help the farmer. Fate turns on a moment, and the pig was about to learn the meaning of those two cruel words "if only…"

Babe leaned over the side of the well to get a better look at what his human was doing. Way down at the bottom, Farmer Hoggett held on to the rope and slowly began lowering the platform.

If only Babe hadn't been so careless…

As the pig leaned over, a block of stone gave way under his feet. The stone tumbled down past Hoggett and fell into the water.

SPLASH!

The farmer looked up to see Babe falling forward onto the platform.

If only the weight of the pig and the pump had not exceeded the weight of the farmer…

Hoggett, still holding on to the rope, was suddenly jerked up into the air like a puppet on a string!

If only the farmer hadn't hit the platform as they passed…

THWACK!

Or jammed his fingers at the top…

OUCH!

If only the pig and the pump had not slipped off at the bottom of the well. Suddenly, the farmer was again heavier than the platform…

BANG! The farmer smashed into the platform on his way down.

And if only the farmer, dazed and bruised, hadn't let go of the rope at the bottom…

Babe looked up to see the platform hurtling toward them. *THUD!* Right onto his master's head.

"Boss!" Babe cried. *"Boss!"* His voice echoed up from the well—which was not nearly as deep as his sorrow.

The next day, the living room of the cozy cottage looked like a hospital. Farmer Hoggett was more bandage than man, encased and weighed down by a complex system of casts and counterweights.

The farmer's wife wrung her hands as she talked to the doctor. Concerned friends, both human and animal, surrounded the quiet farmer in his hour of need.

Everyone glared at the guilty pig as he made his way to his injured friend's side. The cat snarled. Mrs. Hoggett's lips pinched in an angry frown.

Babe could plainly tell what she was thinking. *If only the pig had become pork roast as he was meant to, this never would have happened.*

Babe sat down next to his master's bed, his head bowed meekly. Slowly, Farmer Hoggett raised his bandaged hand and scratched the pig's head.

He doesn't hate me! Babe thought. His eyes shone with tears of joy and remorse. His human was so kind! Even after all the pain Babe had caused him, Hoggett was still his friend.

If there was ever a moment when the pig wished his words could be understood by humans, this was it. In an itty-bitty voice, Babe oinked, "S-s-sorry, Boss."

And in the shadows of the room, three mice sat looking on, one of them singing an old French song. *"Je ne regrette rien,"* the tiny voice squeaked. "I regret nothing." But, of course, the little pig regretted that he had ever been born.

Surely, dear ones, you have noticed that things have a way of going from bad to worse. So it was on Hoggett Farm.

Even before the farmer's accident, the farmer's wife had been ceaselessly busy—bustling, baking, bottling, and pickling. Now she found life even more challenging as she tried to take care of her husband's duties as well.

One of those duties was shearing the sheep.

"Sa-a-ave me!" bleated one victim of her clumsy clipping.

"Ta-a-ake pity!" begged another.

But the farmer's wife was determined to do her best. Her Arthur needed her. It wasn't his fault he'd trusted that...*pig*. But now that they were in this mess...

Mrs. Hoggett released the old sheep she'd been shearing and went after the next.

"How do I look, Fly?" the old sheep asked.

The sheepdog who'd raised Babe as her own was still a bit shaky about following the pig's polite approach to sheep. What do you say to a sheep that looks as if it's been dancing with a Weedwacker?

"Um...well, er..." Fly turned to her husband, Rex. The aged sheepdog, who had taken so long to believe in Babe, tried to ease the old sheep's embarrassment.

"Don't worry," he said. "The difference between a good haircut and a bad haircut is just a couple of weeks...haw-haw."

Just then, Fly spotted something on the horizon. She growled. Mrs. Hoggett stood up and wiped her hands on her apron. She peered across the farmyard at two dark figures holding briefcases.

Mrs. Hoggett gasped as the men started walking toward her. With their pale faces and soulless eyes, they could be from only one place: the bank! No natural disaster—flood, fire, or hurricane—could destroy a farm faster than...men from the bank!

In a panic, Mrs. Hoggett raced back to the cottage. "Oh my gosh! Oh my gosh! Oh, Arthur, deary me!" she panted.

The injured farmer raised his head off his pillow. He watched his wife frantically sift through a pile of papers on the table, her face flushed with exertion. Then her eyes twinkled in triumph. Mrs. Hoggett had found the letter she was looking for. At a speed that defied comprehension, the farmer's wife read:

THE STATE OF EXCITEMENT
PROUDLY PRESENTS
THE GRANDDADDY OF STATE FAIRS
MORE LIVESTOCK, MORE THRILL-RIDES, MORE PRIZES
PLUS THE WORLD'S LARGEST PUMPKIN!

Mrs. Hoggett had no time for overgrown vegetables now! She skipped to the crucial part: "Guest appearance...your pig...sheepherding demonstration...plane tickets...connecting flights...and a generous appearance fee!"

Mrs. Hoggett turned to her husband. "Jumping jam 'n' jellies, Arthur! We just might be able to do it!" By *it*, Mrs. Hoggett meant go to the fair, earn the appearance fee, and pay the men from the bank whatever they needed to let the Hoggetts keep the farm.

Being a man of few words but a great listener, Mr. Hoggett understood his wife. He also agreed. In fact, in his quiet way, the farmer believed that the pig *could* save the farm. After all, if a pig could become a sheepdog, perhaps many things were possible. Hoggett could only hope.

"Pig, Pig, Pig!" Mrs. Hoggett stood in the middle of the yard and called for Babe. Just looking at the barn made her worry about getting hay on her best coat. She brushed at it out of habit.

"Pig!" Mrs. Hoggett called again. "Pig!"

In the field the cow, horse, goats, rooster, sheep, and the sheepdogs Fly and Rex heard the farmer's wife calling.

Fly and Rex looked at each other, then trotted to the barn, where they knew Babe was hiding. The dogs blinked in the hay-and-manure-scented darkness, so different from the bright, fresh day outside. They padded to a large pile of straw in a shadowy corner.

Fly barked, "Come, dear. You're being called."

"Who, me?" a quick voice answered. The straw shuffled as Ferdinand, the skinny duck, emerged from the pile.

Ignoring the nervous duck, Fly spoke gently to the pile of straw. "Babe, you're to go with the boss's wife."

"He's not here," Ferdinand said.

"Babe!" Rex barked. The old sheepdog was as firm as any father.

From under the straw, Babe's tiny voice said, "Babe's not here."

Rex scratched a flea that had been with him for a long time. "You can't undo what's happened, son. But you *can* make up for it," the old dog said.

The straw wiggled. After a moment, Babe came out. "You'll have to excuse me," he said, "but at the moment, I'm feeling a little...you know...forlorn and haunted."

"You can't leave!" Ferdinand quacked. "I need you. You're my lucky pig!"

Fly barked firmly. "Babe, the boss is about to lose the farm. We'll all be sent away."

The horse nodded gravely. "And there's no telling where we'll end up. Not every human is as kind as ours."

Babe felt very small. "But what can *I* do?"

"Nothing!" Ferdinand quacked.

"You're a sheep-pig," said Rex. "A champion, no less. Most likely they want you to herd sheep. Whatever it is...whatever is asked of you...I expect you to do your best."

Babe nodded and took a few tentative steps toward the door.

Ferdinand flapped his skinny wings. "Don't do anything you don't want to do. Pigs have rights, you know!"

In front of the farmhouse, Mrs. Hoggett shouted "PIG!" one last time. Then she turned to her husband, who was propped in a wheelchair on the porch. "Arthur, *you* call the wretched thing!"

Farmer Hoggett spoke in his quiet, gentle voice. "Come, Pig."

Babe felt torn. He looked back at Fly. "I don't want to leave you, Mom."

Fly licked Babe's snout. "You won't be alone, dear. You'll be with the boss's wife."

Babe nodded. Ferdinand freaked. "Oh, sure! The boss's wife! Slice, slice. Chop, chop. You'll be in the company of a serial killer!"

Rex growled, and the duck backpedaled.

"Don't take counsel of your fears, lad," Rex barked.

A cow added, "And never listen to the delirious drivel of a demented duck."

Ferdinand furiously flapped his wings. "I don't recall anybody asking for your opinion."

While they argued, Babe continued walking slowly toward the barn door.

"Do you want to pee before you go?" Fly asked.

"No, thank you," the pig replied as he stepped out into the sunshine and...

...into the arms of Mrs. Hoggett!

"Come now! Chop-chop!" the farmer's wife said as she carried Babe to the truck. Babe was suddenly inside, looking out at the farm through a dusty window.

Ferdinand quacked desperately to Fly. "But I need this pig. He's my good-luck pig! Without him, I'm dead, deceased, lifeless, extinct, a demised duck, a cooked canard!"

Babe looked longingly at Fly. "Can you come with me?" he asked.

The kindly sheepdog shook her head. "I wish I could, dear, but it's you they want."

"Please..." Tears twinkled in the little pig's eyes.

Fly leaned in close. "Stop it now. You're a brave boy, and more often than not in this uncertain world, fortune favors the brave."

Meanwhile, Mrs. Hoggett was giving a few last-minute instructions to two of her friends. They'd be caring for the farmer while she was away. She tried not to think of the many things that might go wrong in her absence.

Finally, she snatched her suitcase and hurried toward the truck. She was halfway there before she realized that she'd forgotten something very important. Mrs. Hoggett turned and blew her husband a kiss.

"Catch it, Arthur," she called.

Arthur Hoggett snatched the kiss out of the air and placed it on his weathered cheek.

Mrs. Hoggett continued on her way to the truck. But before she could get there, the man of few words spoke one. Her name.

"Esme…"

Mrs. Hoggett knew what he was thinking.

"Don't worry, heart," she said. "I'll guard him with my life."

And so the little pig took his leave of all that was home. Once again, he traveled between the green hills, reversing the course he had taken the day of his triumphant parade.

Once again, the sheep bleated from the ridges as he rode by. But this time they were saying, "Save the fa-a-arm, Ba-aabe! Sa-a-ave the FA-A-ARM!"

Their bleats mingled with the gasps of an extremely out-of-shape duck chasing the departing truck. Ferdinand tried to take off as he ranted, "Doom! Doom! No breath, no life. The light…at the end of the tunnel…recedes. Oxygen, oxygen!"

"Sa-a-ave the FA-A-ARM!"

Even as the sheep bleated, two men from the bank put up a sign that read:

MORTGAGE SALE

And so, followed by the catastrophic duck, the

pig and the farmer's wife ventured into the larger world.

The appearance fee, Mrs. Hoggett knew, would keep the bank at bay till Farmer Hoggett was back on his feet. And if luck was on their side, they might just make it.

What follows, dear ones, is an account of their calamitous adventures…and how a kind and steady heart can mend a sorry world.

Chapter Two

Scram!
This Is Not a Farm!

VA-ROOM! The huge jet's giant engines roared to life. In his little cage in the cargo hold, Babe tried to be brave. He sang to himself in a soft, quavering voice, "La, la, la...La, la, la..."

The little pig took a deep breath and tried to sing louder, but the engines drowned out his song.

In the jet's cabin, Mrs. Hoggett watched the flight attendant as she went through the safety instructions. Bored passengers glared at her for wearing her life vest and—*WHOOSH!*—inflating it!

Outside, Ferdinand tapped on the window. But no one noticed the desperate duck. As the jet took off, Ferdinand was left flapping far behind. He flew as hard as his little wings could, but the jet kept get-

15

ting smaller and smaller until it was just a tiny dot in the sky.

Then he heard a chorus of voices behind him. Ferdinand was soon overtaken by a flock of swinging geese singing, *"Pardon me, boys. Is that the cat-that-chewed-your-new-shoes?"*

Ferdinand puffed to the nearest goose, "See that…fat…featherless…flying thing?"

The goose nodded its long neck. Of course he could see the jet.

"Know…where…it's headed?" Ferdinand huffed.

The goose answered in song, *"Yeah, yeah. Follow us!"*

"Er, excuse me…" Babe said, his little snout pressed against the bars of his cage. The cage had just been delivered by conveyor belt to a dimly lit cavern.

Babe addressed the only other living being in the huge room: a hyperactive beagle wearing a jacket with the words DRUG DETECTION printed on it. The dog was sniffing his way through the mountains of luggage one suitcase at a time.

"Excuse me," Babe tried again, "but I was wondering…"

The dog just kept sniffing. "Look, pal, I'm busy."

"I—I—I seem to have lost my human," Babe said. "Sh-sh-she's…"

"Hey! I'm working here! Earning a living, *comprendez?*" The beagle turned and saw Babe for the first time. "Whoa! Ain't you a weird-looking puppy!"

"I'm not a puppy," Babe said. "I am a sheep-pig. And my human is gone and I'm hungry and I'm supposed to save the farm."

"Yeah, yeah. That's truly tragic," the dog barked gruffly. "But you see that long line of stuff here, and all those piles over there? Well, I gotta sniff every doggone one of them. Sniff, sniff, sniff. I'm a sniffer, ya see? A fully qualified, triple-certified sniffer."

The beagle lifted his big, wet nose for Babe to see. "It's all in the hooter, the schnoz, the olfactory instrument," he said. The beagle looked at Babe's snout with its wide, moist tip. "You could be a sniffer with a schnoz like that."

"That's very kind of you," Babe said, "but…"

"Hey! You got something against sniffing?" the beagle asked. "Listen, Fido, it ain't as easy as it looks! It takes a lot of educatin'. Knowin' the smells, knowin' precisely what to sniff…"

"I didn't mean to offend…" Babe said.

"Hold on, I'm just getting to the good part!" said the beagle. "When ya sniff the right smell, y'know what happens? Do ya? Do ya?" the dog asked excitedly.

Babe shook his head.

"You jump up and down and go berserk!" the beagle answered gleefully. "Barkin' beef-bones! You should see the humans come runnin'."

"They do? Why?" Babe asked.

"Beats me, but I get big rewards."

Babe was intrigued. "Rewards?"

"Sure! My heart's desire! Watch this!" The beagle started barking. Right in Babe's face!

Customs officials hurried to see which bag was causing all the fuss. Then they found the bag's owner and stared in surprise.

The customs officer shook his head. "She could be my mom," he said.

The officer's partner agreed. "Yeah. Creepy, isn't it?"

Mrs. Hoggett was quickly surrounded by a group of customs officers. The first approached her cautiously.

"Esme Cordelia Hoggett?" he asked.

"Oh, thank heavens!" Mrs. Hoggett said. She was glad to see the official. She had to find the pig and make their connecting flight!

"Ma'am, we have the pig," the officer said.

"Well, what are we waiting for?" said Mrs. Hoggett. "Come on! Chop-chop! If we miss Flight one-fifteen, we won't make the four-fifteen shuttle. And if we miss the shuttle, we won't arrive on time for the fair. And if we miss the fair, we won't earn the appearance money. And if we don't have the money, the bank won't take 'Sorry, I missed the flight' for an answer…"

Mrs. Hoggett was so busy chattering, she hardly noticed the officers herding her into an interrogation room. Babe sat on the middle of a stainless steel table beneath his own lighted x-ray.

A female officer approached Mrs. Hoggett. "Esme Cordelia Hoggett, we have reason to believe that you may be carrying illegal substances on your person. As an officer of the Drug Enforcement Agency, I am authorized by law to undertake certain procedures…"

Mrs. Hoggett was examined more closely than a prize pig on market day. Of course, it was proved beyond any doubt that Esme Cordelia Hoggett was of virtuous character, but sadly the farmer's wife and pig had missed their all-important connecting flight. And to make matters worse, they were obliged to wait some days for the next flight home. They couldn't go forward, and they couldn't go back. They were stranded at the airport.

Mrs. Hoggett called some hotels. None would take pets!

"It's only a *little* pig," she explained to the first hotel clerk. The phone clicked. Mrs. Hoggett tried again. "Well, it's more of a dog, really." Another hotel operator hung up. Mrs. Hoggett tried yet again. "But he's practically human!" she wailed.

No hotel, it seemed, would open its doors to the farmer's wife and pig. Mrs. Hoggett fell asleep on a bench with her arms cradling Babe. The once-bustling airport was now deserted, except for them, the night cleaner, and the security guard.

"Move on, lady. No animals in the airport," the guard said gruffly.

Mrs. Hoggett yawned. "You don't understand. We've nowhere to…"

The guard understood. He just didn't care. "Scram!" he shouted. "This is not a farm."

Mrs. Hoggett spent the rest of the night in the deserted airport avoiding the security guard. Toward dawn, the resourceful farmer's wife devised a disguise. The deception worked on many busy commuters. Without a second glance, they bustled past the plump woman cradling a large baby in her arms.

But, alas, the security guard was not so easily fooled. He tapped Mrs. Hoggett on the shoulder. She looked up from the baby snuggled against her shoulder. Babe's twinkly gaze was as innocent as a newborn's. But his long snout and floppy ears made for a very peculiar-looking infant.

The guard was not impressed by Mrs. Hoggett's resourcefulness. He herded her and her pig out onto the noisy street.

Horns honked. Brakes squealed. Limousines

swarmed like busy beetles. The acrid smell of exhaust filled the air.

Mrs. Hoggett took a deep breath and prepared to set off into the chaos. But before she could, the night cleaner trotted up. He handed Mrs. Hoggett a slip of paper:

THE FLEALANDS HOTEL
349 RANDOM CANAL

"I didn't give you this," he said.

Mrs. Hoggett studied the pink round face of the stranger and wondered what had provoked this unexpected act of kindness. Small, twinkly eyes blinked back at her with the loving look of a well-fed pig! Before she could thank him, the little man was lost in the flock of commuters.

Armed with only the note, Mrs. Hoggett set off. She clutched her battered suitcase and led her pig on a leash across a grand plaza the likes of which the two of them had never seen.

If you've lived all your life in the modern metropolis, you may no longer be impressed by the zuzz and the buzz and the boom-bang-clang. But imagine if you came from Hoggett Hollow, a little green valley somewhere just to the left of the twentieth century...

Babe's trotters clicked on the pavement. His ears perked up at the mixture of sounds. Dogs of every breed, from pampered pedigrees to the lowest alley mutt, moved to the street's snappy beat. Through a forest of legs, Babe saw police horses prance proudly by. They were nothing like the humble horse back on the farm.

Before long, the streets changed. The slip of paper led Mrs. Hoggett toward the beach. The breezy promenade bustled with every kind of human: musclemen, motorcycle cops, bikers, in-line skaters, beach bums, and street vendors.

Finally, wide streets gave way to a crooked maze of narrow canals and bridges. Mrs. Hoggett had reached her goal. She stared from the piece of paper clutched in her fingers to the ramshackle four-story building known as the Flealands Hotel.

Chapter Three

What Kind of Establishment Do You Think This Is?

Mrs. Hoggett knocked on the door. A face appeared behind a dusty pane of glass.

"I need a room for myself and…er…the…er…wee pig," Mrs. Hoggett said.

The door was flung open, and the landlady stepped out. "Are you crazy?" she shouted. "Animals in here? What makes you think we take animals?"

"Oh…but…" Mrs. Hoggett didn't know what to say.

"What kind of establishment do you think this is?" the landlady snapped. "Well, it isn't! Am I aware of the city codes and regulations? Yes! Do I support the new ordinances? Most definitely. Am I one to break the law? Absolutely not!"

She slammed the door.

Mrs. Hoggett didn't know what else to do. She knocked again.

"Are you hearing-impaired?" the landlady squawked. "Go away!"

Mrs. Hoggett stood on the corner and looked around. Back in Hoggett Hollow, Esme always knew where she was going. But here…

"Oh…well…er…but…mmm…gosh…I never… um…goodness…yes…dearie me…" she muttered to herself as she walked past the side of the hotel.

"Psst!"

Mrs. Hoggett turned and saw the landlady waving to her.

"M-m-me?" Mrs. Hoggett was completely confused. The landlady pulled her and Babe into a shadowy alley.

"How long do you want to stay?" the landlady whispered.

"Er…two days," Mrs. Hoggett replied.

"Will an attic room do?" the landlady asked. She led them to the hotel's back door.

Mrs. Hoggett was confused. "But I thought you said…"

"Oh, that was just for the neighbors," the landlady explained. "Heartless meanies. Where do they expect these poor creatures to go?" The landlady looked at Babe. "Is he house-trained?"

"Oh, yes. Just like you and me," Mrs. Hoggett assured her.

The landlady led them inside the Flealands Hotel. As they climbed a rickety flight of stairs, the eccentric woman rattled on. "Do we provide meals? No. But is there a convenience store? Yes, two blocks south. And what is the golden rule? Never answer the front door. Why? It might be an inspector. Mind that step."

On the first landing, Babe glanced through a half-open door. From the darkness, someone was watching them!

On the next landing, Babe turned to see two dogs peeking out at him: Nigel, an English bulldog, and Alan, a Neapolitan mastiff. The dogs wore matching blankets with a tasteful floral pattern.

A third dog, Flealick, shot out from between Nigel and Alan. Flealick's crippled back legs were mounted on wheels. A checkered flag waved from the top of an aerial attached to the contraption.

Flealick sniffed Babe up and down. "Canine... er...no. Don't tell me, I'll get it."

Nigel, the bulldog, whispered, "Flealick! Come back! We don't know where it's been. Do we, Alan?"

The mastiff shook his massive black head. "No, Nigel, we don't."

Flealick kept sniffing. "I need a clue. It's my nose. Sinusitis!" The small dog sniffed even harder.

"Feline. Oh, no, you're a cat!"

"Do I look like a cat?" Babe asked.

Flealick squinted. "Not sure. It's my eyes. Cataracts."

He sniffed again. "If you're a cat, you've got no business on this floor! Get that? No felines on this floor!"

The curious crippled dog tried to follow Babe up the stairs, but his wheels got stuck. Flealick wheezed with his efforts.

"Good heavens, his heart condition!" Nigel fretted. "He'll kill himself, won't he, Alan?"

"Yes, Nigel," agreed the mastiff.

As they neared the top floor, Babe heard a chorus of cats humming. The landlady rattled on to Mrs. Hoggett. "Where's the pay phone? In the foyer. Local calls only. Where does the little piggy stay at all times? In the room. Where does the dear little fella do his necessaries? In the kitty litter. Who empties it? You do." She unlocked the door to the attic room. "Any questions?"

"Oh, yes, my husband," Mrs. Hoggett replied. "Where do I make a long-distance call?"

Mrs. Hoggett placed a picture of Arthur on the bedside table. She grabbed her purse and turned to Babe. "Stay, Pig. Stay," she said firmly.

Then she pulled the door shut behind her. Babe

jumped onto a chair to look out the window. The city stretched as far as his eyes could see: skyscrapers, smokestacks, statues, fountains, a huge building shaped like a gigantic shell, a great sweeping bridge, a towering clock. Their outlines shone against the twinkling glow of the fantastic city.

As Babe looked out across this vast habitat, abundant with humans and other creatures, he wondered when he would see his first sheep. Then the thought occurred to him: Maybe it wouldn't be sheepherding. Maybe something else was required of him. Whatever the case, in this place with its dark corners and endless possibilities, the pig felt sure he would find a way to redeem himself.

Behind the contemplative pig, the door opened quietly. A tiny monkey scampered into the room and looked around with large, shiny eyes.

"Um…can I help you?" the pig asked politely.

The tiny monkey, whose name was Tug, grabbed the photograph of Farmer Hoggett and dropped it in Mrs. Hoggett's battered suitcase. His reply sounded like nonsense to Babe, but Tug made perfect sense—if you knew how to talk backward. "Esaelp tnod pots em gniod ym boj," the monkey chattered. (*Please don't stop me doing my job.*)

"Beg your pardon?" Babe asked.

Instead of answering, Tug shut the suitcase and shoved it off the bed.

"What are you doing?" Babe demanded.

The three little mice who had hitched a ride inside the suitcase scrambled out as Tug pulled the bag out the door.

"Wait a minute!" Babe ran after the departing monkey.

Tug tossed the suitcase down to the next landing. *THUMP, BUMP!* Then he leaped after it.

"Hey!" Babe called after him. "That belongs to the boss's wife!"

Tug was already on the next landing when Babe passed the room with the curious crippled dog. Flealick wheeled out of his room, snuffling and squinting. "Whoa, whoa! If you're not a cat, stay and chat," he barked in a friendly tone.

Nigel and Alan watched from behind the safety of the door.

Babe did not stop in his pursuit of the suitcase. "Sorry," he called over his shoulder. "Don't mean to be rude…"

Tug threw the suitcase down the stairs and rode it like a surfboard to the next landing. Babe tore after him as Flealick called, "Don't get out much nowadays. On account of Nige and Al and their nerves, and me on account of my hips. But don't be a stranger now!"

Babe was not listening. He was too busy keeping up with the monkey. Tug dragged the suitcase

through a door, then slammed it in the pig's face.
BANG!

"Hey! Open up!" Babe called. "Please, can you
open this door?"

The door opened to reveal a creature even more
amazing than the little monkey. Babe gaped at a very
pregnant chimpanzee wearing a pretty dress.

"You got a problem, sweetie?" the chimp asked.
Her name was Zootie.

Babe stared in utter confusion. This furry being
was clearly an animal, yet she was dressed like a
human! "You…um…I…er…" the pig stammered.

"Who is it, honey?" a deep voice asked. Babe
looked past Zootie and saw her husband, Bob. The
male chimp was also dressed like a human. He
lounged on a couch and did not take his eyes off the
flickering images on a TV screen.

Zootie looked at Babe. "It's…er…kind of a
baldy, pinky, whitey thingy." She blew her gum into
a pink bubble.

"Show him in," Bob said amiably.

Babe entered. "I would like the bag back," he
said.

"Hey, pinkess," Bob said. He pointed at Tug.
"Look at the little guy. You wanna break his heart?"

Tug started to cry. "Ili eb etutitsed no eht…
steerts…" (*I'll be destitute on the streets.*)

"But it doesn't belong to him," Babe said.

Bob was unmoved. "All I know is what I see. Tug comes in with the bag, just doing his job collecting stuff, and you barge in here accusicating and making demandments. I didn't see you with the bag. Who's to say it belongs to *you?*"

Babe had never heard such nonsense. "I'm definitely not leaving without that bag."

A smaller chimp sporting a bow tie and checkered pants took off a set of earphones. This was Easy, Bob's younger brother. "I don't think my big brother, Bob Boppaluba the Big Banana, has finished 'splaining how things work around here," Easy said.

Babe faced all three chimpanzees. He took a firm tone with them, the way Fly addressed sheep. "I have to warn you. I may be small, but I can be ferocious if provoked."

The little pig was surprised when the chimps backed off. Then a deep voice rumbled behind him. "And what have we here?"

Babe turned to see a pair of polished shoes, topped by immaculate spats. Above the spats were the neat pants and coat of a butler, a butler who happened to be a huge orangutan!

Bob answered the orangutan's question. "We're in a negotiation with this naked pink individual."

"Yeah, he's of foreign extraction, your honor," Zootie said earnestly before blowing another bubble.

"Possibly even an alien," Easy added.

The orangutan, whose name was Thelonius, thundered, "You drooling imbeciles! This is an omnivorous mammal of the order Ungulata. An inconsequential species with no other purpose than to be eaten by humans. This lowly, handless, deeply unattractive mud-lover is a pig!"

Zootie had heard of pigs but had never actually seen one. "Oh, so *that's* kinda what they sorta look like."

Babe did not appreciate the orangutan's tone. "For your information, I'm a sheep-pig, and I've been sent to save the farm. And come to think of it, I should be saving the farm right now! And...if you can't say anything nice, don't say anything at all!"

"Silence, you rude piece of pork!" Thelonius countered.

Bob liked the idea of food. "So...will this little pink lunchness, you know, fulfill his destiny, nutritionally speaking?"

"We shall see," Thelonius replied.

Babe shifted nervously on his trotters. "I feel very uncomfortable with this conversation. I want my bag back, and I want it now. Please get out of my way."

To Babe's surprise, Thelonius and the chimps backed off. Babe turned and saw why. A human dressed in a stained, wrinkled clown costume had come into the room. The bright colors of the clown's suit contrasted unpleasantly with the sickly pallor of his face. The clown, whose name was Fugly Floom, gnawed a greasy drumstick and stared at the pig.

Suddenly, there came a loud noise from the hall. "Uncle Fugly! Uncle Fugly!" the landlady cried.

The clown quickly picked up the pig and dropped him in a trunk. Then he stepped out of the room.

The landlady and a very worried Mrs. Hoggett came running down the stairs. "There's been a theft upstairs. Can you imagine?" the landlady said.

Fugly Floom scrounged up the dregs of his charm as his niece introduced him to the farmer's wife. "Esme Hoggett, Fugly Floom. Uncle Fugly, Esme Hoggett."

"Perhaps we should call the police," Mrs. Hoggett suggested.

"No!" the landlady said. "Have you forgotten? No police, no authorities! Heaven forbid. That would be the end of this place. Surely you understand?"

"Oh dear," Mrs. Hoggett fretted. "I just phoned my Arthur to tell him at least his pig was safe, and now I've gone and lost the blessed little thing."

Inside Fugly's room, Babe popped his head out of the trunk. "That's my human!" he squealed.

"Shh!" Thelonius hissed.

"But she—" Babe began.

Thelonius slammed the trunk lid shut.

Out on the landing, Mrs. Hoggett was saying, "The clothes…I don't care about the clothes. But the pig? I can't go home without the pig!"

Fugly Floom drooled and gesticulated. Somehow his niece understood. "Approximately five minutes ago he saw something that looked like a pig exit this establishment. Where did it go? Left on Canal Street and then in the direction of the beach."

The three mice peeked over the banister and watched Mrs. Hoggett hurry out of the Flealands Hotel.

"Listen!" one of them hissed.

Three pairs of ears heard a mysterious humming. They followed the sound to a door down the hall where they found…hundreds of cats singing "Three Blind Mice" in flawless harmony!

> *"They all ran after the farmer's wife,*
> *who cut off their tails with a carving knife…"*

Chilled to their whiskers, the mice ran squeaking and eeking back to the relative safety of the attic room.

Chaos Theory

"Pig...Pig...PIG!" Mrs. Hoggett cried as she searched the crowded promenade. All kinds of people were out that day, including two motorcycle cops!

"Pig, pig, pig, pig!" she called as she walked past them.

Pedestrians smirked, never imagining that the distressed woman might actually be calling for a pig and not shouting insults at officers of the law. If only searching for a pig in the city couldn't be so easily misconstrued...

With a *vroom* of their engines, the cops took off after Mrs. Hoggett.

The good woman did not notice her pursuers. In fact, Mrs. Hoggett was so intent on finding the pig that she wandered down a lonely back street.

If only the farmer's wife had been more wary of dark alleys.

"Pig, pig, pig…" Mrs. Hoggett called, drawing the attention of a street gang. One of the members was dancing on in-line skates. His large body moved in perfect time to the music.

Until he heard Mrs. Hoggett. "Hey, what?" he asked her.

"I'm looking for my husband's pig," the farmer's wife explained.

"Yeah, right. What ya got in that bag?" the dancer demanded.

Mrs. Hoggett froze. Then, not knowing what else to do, she started dancing! For a moment, the bizarre strategy worked. While the man gaped in wonder, Mrs. Hoggett ran!

But just before she could get out of reach, he grabbed her handbag. Mrs. Hoggett refused to let go of the bag. But neither would the dancer. The farmer's wife ran, dragging the man along on his blades. The rest of his gang followed.

When she reached the end of the alley, Mrs. Hoggett swung the dancer directly into the path of the motorcycle cops. The crashing cops caused a chain reaction: Cyclists, skaters, and skateboarders collided in a chaotic screech of out-of-control wheels!

One skateboarder swerved into a ladder. Two

workmen were using that ladder to glue up a giant poster. The men fell, dragging half the poster with them. And the glue came glopping down on top of Mrs. Hoggett!

As if that was not bad enough, a beautiful woman skater wearing nothing but a bikini swept past the farmer's wife with a *swoosh* of skates and snatched her handbag.

As wet glue slowly slid over every inch of her, Mrs. Hoggett wondered how things could possibly get worse. Then sirens blared. Lights flashed. And a police sergeant strode toward her. He flipped open his official notebook and regarded her with a skeptical stare.

Dear ones, let it not be said that Mrs. Hoggett alone enjoyed the excitement of the city. At that very moment, Babe was fidgeting behind a makeshift stage in a hospital ward, waiting to make his debut!

Under the spotlight, Fugly Floom popped the cork of a giant papier-mâché champagne bottle. Huge soap bubbles drifted over the heads of giggling children wearing hospital gowns and bandages.

Tug's tiny fingers poked at the bubbles. Thelonius held up a sign bearing the phrase:

A CHAMPAGNE DINNER

Bob and Zootie sat at a candlelit table in front of

a painted backdrop proclaiming:

THE FABULOUS FLOOMS
AND THEIR
AMAZING APES!

Babe was nervous! The blank eyes of a papier-mâché pig stared at him. This was even worse than waiting for the National Sheepdog Trials to begin!

Easy sat calmly atop a magician's box. A veteran of many such shows, the young chimp assured the pig, "Just do what they told you. You'll be okay."

"But...but..."

Suddenly, the pig was rolling! Fugly Floom wheeled the magician's box on stage.

Easy sawed the "pig" in half. Mechanical legs pumped furiously as Babe's bewildered head poked from the front of the box.

Thelonius held up another sign:

SPECIALTY OF THE HOUSE

As Fugly split the box in two, a chain of pork sausages spilled out. The next sign instructed:

LAUGHTER AND APPLAUSE

The audience obeyed.

Thelonius flipped another sign that said simply: HAM.

Easy reappeared with a silver domed platter.

Fugly placed the platter on the table and lifted the lid to reveal Babe's head!

Forgetting their various ailments, the children giggled. Fugly started to walk away from the table, but Bob grabbed the clown by his trick suspenders. Fugly made it halfway across the stage before the suspenders snapped him back to the table.

Bob pointed to the restless pig as Thelonius displayed the next card:

TOO RARE

Fugly replaced the silver dome and whisked away the platter. Babe peeked up through the hole in the table. "How am I doing?" he asked.

Zootie pushed Babe's head back down out of view. "Not now, sweetie!" the pregnant chimp shushed the pig. "Not now!"

The last sign proclaimed PARTING SHOT as Fugly placed a ball in a small cannon. Babe crept out from under the table. "Excuse me," he asked Thelonius. "When do I get my reward? You know…my heart's desire?"

"Get back under the table!" Thelonius commanded.

Fugly lit the fuse and aimed the cannon at the audience. The clown turned his back and put his fingers in his ears.

Easy turned the cannon to face Fugly. The audience giggled with anticipation.

Babe was trotting back to his place under the table just as Fugly Floom turned toward the cannon. The clown tripped over the pig, and the large flaming match in Fugly's hand ignited the stage curtains!

Frightened by the flames, Zootie clambered up onto the sprinkler system. Bob followed, knocking over the backdrop in his haste. Props flew everywhere!

BOOM! The cannon exploded, shooting a bright spray of confetti and streamers. Triggered by the smoke, the sprinkler system sprayed water over everything. Alarms blared! People and primates scattered in all directions.

Ever mindful of his honored human, Thelonius helped Fugly to his feet.

Babe watched, frozen with fear, as the papier-mâché pig's head tumbled toward him and stopped only inches from his snout!

Chapter Five

Fortune Favors the Brave...Right?

Babe's gut growled like an angry monster. For the past hour, the patient pig had watched Fugly Floom stuff his face in the kitchen of his Flealands Hotel room. Ripped-up wrappers and flattened cans lay among dirty plates and silverware.

Babe had shut his eyes to cut off the terrible sight. But he could not shut his ears to the sound of countless cans being opened, crinkly wrappers torn, whipped cream squirted, and mouthfuls hastily chewed as the clown gobbled down the food.

Babe's sensitive snout had been teased by the smell of greasy hamburgers and piping-hot french fries. Capping off the ravenous pig's evening of torture was Fugly Floom's dessert. After the cakes, shakes, puddings, and pies, Fugly still had an appetite for some candy.

The clown's adoring butler held a heart-shaped box of fine chocolates out to Fugly. Thelonius waited stiffly at attention while the clown tried to decide between caramel and truffle, before settling on both.

In seconds, the chocolates were just a smear. His meal concluded, the clown rose from the table with a resounding *burp!* Thelonius gently guided him into the other room, where the comfy couch waited.

While the loyal orangutan was in the living room, the chimps edged toward the chocolate box he had left on the table. Bob's pink-tipped fingers reached toward the heart-shaped cardboard and almost brushed it when...

A huge auburn paw swiped the box away. Thelonius put the lid carefully back on the box and carried it to the living room.

Meanwhile, the chimps sifted through the pile of wrappers and sauce-smeared plates for any scrap of nourishment.

Babe trotted across the slippery kitchen floor to the table. "Any food? Any leftovers?" he called up to the chimps eagerly. his stomach rumbled loudly.

Easy glanced down and tossed a jar off the table. It rolled toward the desperate pig.

"Hey. What'd you do that for?" Bob asked.

Easy shrugged. "I dunno. His belly's rumbling."

Bob frowned. "We look after our own first."

"Listen to your big brother. He's, y'know…ya big brother," Zootie advised.

Babe did not hear the discussion. His snout was deep inside the peanut butter jar. But he still couldn't reach the last lick of sweet, sticky goo.

Babe nudged the jar into the living room, where it bumped against the couch. The hungry pig jammed his nose deeper into the jar, which was now braced against a sofa leg.

Babe grunted with effort. He still couldn't reach the peanut butter! And now he tried to pull his face out of the jar. But he couldn't. He was stuck!

Glancing up, Babe saw Thelonius gently remove Fugly Floom's shoes. The furry butler lifted the clown's feet onto a footstool and lovingly tucked a blanket around the man's shoulders.

Fugly Floom did not look good. Well, dear ones, Fugly had not looked close to anything resembling good for many years. But that night, following his feast, the clown looked even worse than usual.

Thelonius tenderly placed the chocolate box on the clown's chest. The three chimps watched the fate of the candy from the kitchen door.

Babe did not care what happened to the chocolates. For the first time in over an hour, the pig forgot he was hungry. He had a jar stuck on his face!

If ever a pig wished he had hands, this was the moment. He shook his snout up and down and from side to side. But the jar would not budge!

Babe's muffled grunts of frustration finally caught Thelonius's attention. The orangutan pulled off the jar.

Babe's anger came gushing out. "Nothing's happening the way it's supposed to," he said. "I did everything that was asked of me. I got in the box. I put my head through the hole. I was charming. So where's my reward? You said I'd get a reward. Everyone's counting on me. 'Specially my human. She'll be back very soon, so I better get my reward. Where's my—"

Thelonius rammed the jar back on Babe's snout. The pig started to protest, but then he heard a hiss.

"Psst!" Bob beckoned Babe to the kitchen. "I know where your reward is," the chimp whispered.

"Oo doo?" Babe's voice was muffled by the jar.

"Oodliedoodles of reward," Bob promised. "And I know exactly how to get it…"

Bob pointed to a hole in the ceiling. Easy started to giggle. Zootie nudged him. Easy clamped his hand over his mouth.

"'N it'll 'elp saaae de faarr?" Babe's garbled words came through the fog of breath clouding the jar.

"What? Save the *what?*" Bob demanded crossly.

"Saae de faarr! De faaarrr!" Babe squealed.

"That thingy, you know…" Zootie said.

"De faaar!" Babe grunted through the jar.

Bob didn't care what the pig was talking about. "Yeah, yeah, we know," he said. "And it's gonna happen. Truly-ruly. But if you wanna save the 'fun,' you do exactly as I say, okay?"

Babe nodded. He had to save the farm. And he had to get this jar off his head—not necessarily in that order!

Finally, Bob reached toward the pig's smeared prison. "Now I'm gonna take this off…"

Babe gasped in the fresh, peanut-free air! He hastened to express himself, "Actually, it was save the f—"

"Uh-uh! Not a word." Bob held up his hand and nodded toward the living room, where Thelonius was watching TV and his beloved human was sleeping fitfully.

The chimps built a tower of junk in the corner of the cluttered kitchen. Slowly the pile of old newspapers, boxes, and an ancient TV climbed toward the hole.

"I'd go up, only I'm pregnant," Zootie said.

"I'd go up, only I'm afraid of heights," Easy explained.

"I'd go, only I'm collapsaphobic." Bob wasn't sure what that meant, but he figured it sounded good enough to fool the pig.

Babe craned his neck way back to stare at the distant opening. The hole looked awfully high up.

He swallowed hard. His empty stomach rumbled aggressively. Babe recalled Fly's wisdom.

"Well, um, fortune favors the brave. Right? Have you heard that?" he asked.

Bob nodded impatiently. "Indeed, my little braveness. Absoposolutely."

Bob nudged the pig toward the tower. Babe began a slow and perilous climb…

BA-RIIIIING! In the living room, Thelonius lifted the receiver and listened.

"*I promised them a good show, a safe show, ya MORON! Whatever gave you the crazy idea of using a live pig, YA MATZO BALL!*"

The clown sat up groggily and groaned. Thelonius held the phone a few inches from the clown's ear, close enough for him to hear, but not enough to cause severe pain.

"*I always stuck by ya! When your own parents tossed you out of the act, I stuck by ya. When no other clown would touch you with a ten-foot pogo stick, I stuck by ya!*"

The tiny, angry voice droned on.

"*Henceforth, hereafter, I am no longer responsible for what I laughingly call your career. Floom, you're through, kaput, finished, finito!*"

Fugly dropped the receiver into the nearby fishbowl. The plastic palace and few inches of water were not much. But they were all the feisty little fish had.

"Hey!" the fish shouted up at the thoughtless giants. "I'm swimmin' here! *I'm swimmin' here!*"

Thelonius pulled out the receiver, shook the water from it, and placed it back on the cradle. Then the huge ape bent down to the tiny fish.

"My apologies," he whispered.

"I might come down now." Babe's voice was almost as small as the tiny fish's. The pig balanced on a chair that swayed like a seesaw.

"No, no! You're doing fine!" Bob called.

"To be perfectly honest, I'm s-s-stuck!" The pig was rigid with fear.

"Don't look down!" Easy coached. "Just don't look down!"

So, of course, Babe looked down. His trotters teetertottered! He held his breath and felt the world spin around him. Suddenly, he was back at the edge of the well, nudging that fateful stone out of place. Bob's voice called him back from the brink. "You're almost there."

The brave little pig tried to take heart. "C-c-closer to the t-t-top than the b-b-bottom…huh?"

Ever so slowly, Babe inched his way toward the top of the tower. Who would have guessed that this plump, ungainly creature could have been capable of such grace? And yet, through sheer determination, Babe made it!

The pig held his breath until the swaying finally

stopped. Only then did he dare to whisper, "N-n-now what?"

Bob hesitated for a moment, letting the excitement build. "Well..." He winked at Easy, who was slipping out the door. Then he said, "This happens." Unseen by Babe, Bob gave the teetering tower a shove! The tower swayed wildly one way...then the other...

Babe's eyes widened! He held his breath and tried to keep his balance. But the ladder of junk was as doomed to fall as a stone loosened from the rim of a well. Babe tumbled, squealing, down the toppling tower of trash and out an open window!

The plucky pig clung to an awning hanging over the canal. Tug watched as Babe scrambled to keep his footing.

In the kitchen, the tower of trash crashed! Thelonius leaped up and stormed into the room.

"Well, it was like this..." Bob stammered. "The naked pink individual comes in here intent on doing this stupid trick."

"Yeah, stupid trick," Zootie chimed in.

"Don't ask us to interpolate what's going on in that strange little head," Bob said. "But it strikes me as very destructive behavior."

Easy appeared in the kitchen door, one hand casually behind his back. "Perhaps it's a cry for help," he said.

"And where is the delinquent swine now?" Thelonius demanded.

Zootie didn't know what to say. "Y'know. He's around...he's um..."

Outside the window, Babe's trotters slipped. The pig squealed for help as he slipped down the awning and into the canal with a loud splash.

"...swimming," Zootie concluded.

Bob shrugged. "Go figure."

Thelonius rubbed his temples, then took a deep breath. The orangutan felt a headache coming on. "I will not allow whatever mad mischief you have concocted here tonight to ruin another lovely evening. I am going back inside to attend to Himself. You are going to tidy up. This is a civilized household. Tranquillity will prevail."

The chimps waited for Thelonius to go back into the living room. Then Easy pulled his hand out from behind his back. His nimble, furry fingers held Fugly Floom's box of chocolates. The chimps gave a hushed cheer and traded high-fives.

In the canal below, Babe came to the surface spluttering. This was not good, clean country water. The surface was scummed with an oily slick. Gum wrappers, chunks of garbage, and things too terrible to mention floated in the sluggish current.

Babe did not like swimming. But Fly had taught him how, just in case. The little pig dog-paddled through the cold water toward the hotel. The tiny monkey who had watched his struggle opened the Flealands' front door.

Meanwhile, the chimps' cheer had proved short-lived. Within seconds, Thelonius was back in the kitchen. Zootie held a chocolate close to her mouth. The orangutan reached out his hand.

"Please, just one, just one, one, one, one little oney..." Zootie begged.

But Thelonius took her chocolate, then reached for Easy's. "It's not fair!" Easy protested. "Why take it all out on us?"

"We're being victimated against. He's an inhu-maniac!" Bob added.

Thelonius's head throbbed. How could he explain Himself's mysterious ways to a mere chimp? "Himself doesn't want you to suffer. He just wants you to learn restraint, discipline. He wants you to elevate yourselves!"

The orangutan reached for Bob's chocolate.

Suddenly, Bob tossed the candy in his mouth and held the box behind his back!

The strong orangutan easily pulled Bob's arm to the front. But the hungry chimp refused to sur-render.

The arm wrestling raged on as Babe barreled in, wet, shaking, huffing, puffing, and getting angrier by the minute.

"Hey! Hey! Anyone notice that I'm dripping wet over here? Anyone wonder why?" the pig asked.

No one noticed except Easy. "I'd keep my trap shut if I were you," the young chimp warned as Thelonius finally forced Bob to drop the chocolate box.

"Why do you always side with the human?" Zootie asked Thelonius.

"Yeah, you ashamed of what you are?" Easy jumped in.

Thelonius frowned. "While we were hunched over, dragging our knuckles, humans were creating all this. They are the supreme species. They make the world work."

"Well, right now the supreme Himself couldn't tie his own shoes," Bob said.

"Yeah, why is he always drooling?" Easy wondered.

"I'm sure he has his own good reasons," the orangutan asserted.

Babe asked, "Does he have a good reason for not giving me my reward?!"

"Does he have a good reason when he does this?" Bob demanded as he let out a huge burp!

Zootie imitated Fugly's snore while Easy blew raspberries. The three chimps were soon given over to the lowest form of monkey business. Bob even dared to take off his jacket!

"PUT YOUR CLOTHES BACK ON, YOU MINDLESS KNUCKLE-WALKER!" Thelonius thundered. "You don't deserve his...benevolence! *He* put the very clothes on our backs. He taught us to walk upright. He freed our hands for higher works!"

"BUT HE DIDN'T GIVE ME MY REWARD!" Babe squealed.

Thelonius went ape! He tossed the hapless pig out the window. With a loud splash, Babe was back in the foul canal.

"Who's next?" the orangutan inquired.

By the time the exhausted pig had made his way back to the kitchen, the chimps were obediently cleaning up.

"Just tell me. There is no reward, is there?" he asked.

Zootie looked up from mopping.

"Was there ever such a thing?" Babe asked.

Zootie said, "Oh, little pink thingy. This is the city. As Bob always says... *What* do you say, Bob?"

"It's all illusory," he answered. "It's ill and it's for losers."

Babe didn't quite know what Bob meant, but it sounded sad and cynical.

"No guarantees, my little pork pie," Zootie went on. "It's a dog-eat-dog world and there's not enough dog to go around. So you look after number whatsy. Get my drift?"

Babe thought for a moment, then replied, "I'm not a pork pie." He turned and walked slowly out the door.

Zootie called after him, "Whatever you say, cutie pie."

Babe didn't know what he was anymore. But he knew what he wasn't! "I'm not a cutie pie. I'm not any kind of pie…I'm a pig on a mission."

The small, determined animal took refuge in his attic room, where he stared out into the night. The city twinkled below like a vast fairy castle. The tall towers of huge apartment buildings glowed with the flickering lights of many TV sets, against which humans' silhouettes moved like shadow puppets. A mournful saxophone echoed from a roof. Sea gulls soared and wheeled in currents high above floodlit skyscrapers.

It's tough if you're a pig alone in the city. With each small step, you seem to slide a long way back. It leaves you empty. And whom do you turn to? Where was the boss's wife?

Babe thought it might help if he could recall Fly and Rex and their steadfast words. And he tried, really hard. But the little pig could barely even remember the face of his beloved boss. The farm was fading…it had become just a comforting dream… an echo…

The three mice crooned a tune made famous by

Elvis, the immortal king of rock 'n' roll:

*"Are you lonesome tonight? Do you miss me tonight?
Are you sorry we drifted apart?"*

Suddenly, the night exploded with color! Babe
blinked at the wondrous display of fireworks. Never,
except perhaps for a heaping plate of Mrs. Hoggett's
corn bread stuffing, had he ever seen a more beautiful sight.

The next morning, Babe woke to loud thumps and
voices from downstairs. He went out to the landing
and saw medics taking Fugly Floom out of his room.
The clown's face was covered by an oxygen mask. An
IV dripped into his limp arm. A heart monitor
beeped at irregular intervals.

The landlady held her uncle's hand. She looked
very worried.

The hotel, usually so alive with meowing, woofing, and other animal sounds, was eerily silent. The
residents had vanished at the first sight of strangers.

The landlady stopped at the door to throw a coat
over her nightgown. Thelonius stepped from the
shadows, and the landlady paused to gaze into the
orangutan's frightened eyes. Then she looked away
quickly.

When the door closed behind the landlady, the
other animals emerged from hiding. To everyone's
surprise, Thelonius suddenly swung up the stairs,

from balcony to balcony, once more the powerful trapeze artist of the jungle.

The orangutan swung toward Babe. The startled pig stepped away. The brooding beast swung right past him, finally stopping at the tower window above the hotel attic.

A siren wailed as the ambulance left for the hospital. Thelonius's huge shoulders drooped.

Babe did not know what to do. Easy walked up to the old ape. "Are we okay, Thelonius?"

The orangutan answered in a hoarse whisper, "I couldn't wake him. I tried, but he wouldn't wake up."

"He'll be back," Easy said. "Himself always comes back."

Thelonius looked away. Babe went back to his room and crawled under the bed.

Perhaps, dear ones, you have forgotten Ferdinand. The demented duck had not given up on his quest. The frantic fowl had used every trick up his feathers to reach the bustling metropolis and find his lucky pig!

The journey had not been easy. After flapping his heart out with the singing, swinging geese, Ferdinand had hitched a ride with a sympathetic pelican—who, unfortunately, dropped the duck among the targets of a busy shooting range. Ferdinand's goose was very nearly cooked!

Gunshots still ringing in his ears, the exhausted duck sheltered in the arms of a stone angel atop a Gothic church. He called feebly with the last of his strength, "Pig...p-pig..."

Chapter Six

A Murderous Heart

By that night, the only voice Babe could hear was the insistent moan of his grumbling stomach…

Rrrgghh…rrrrgghhh…ooooff….

Babe's belly made such a fuss that he began to believe it was talking to him. The rumble became words! *"Foooood…fooood…ooh, food!"*

Then Babe heard another voice. Bob said, "Food. Anybody got any food?"

Babe looked down through the banister. He saw Bob calling up from the bottom floor. "Hey, dogs! You got any edibles? Any nibbly-dibblies?"

Flealick appeared on the dogs' landing. "We got a carpet with some nice spaghetti stains."

"But we can't keep licking the carpet. Can we, Alan?" fretted Nigel the bulldog.

"No, Nigel," the mastiff agreed.

"Hey, cats! Cats! Got any food?" Bob yelled.

Four cats opened a door near Babe. They each sang in turn, then together in harmony, like a barbershop quartet. "No, no, no, no. We have no food."

Zootie looked at Bob. Her husband nodded. "Well, then, I'm gonna get proactivated. I know where there's food-a-plentiful."

Zootie was alarmed. "We're going outside without a human? Could be sorta dangerous, in a lethal kinda way."

"We'll stick to the shadows, honey. It's coolness," Bob assured her.

From the attic landing, Babe watched the chimps leave. Thelonius slumped in the tower window, as still as a stone gargoyle.

Babe could not stay still. He had to eat. Now!

The chimps crept between the streetlights along the canal like the spies Bob watched on TV. Their reflections floated on the smooth blackness of the quiet water.

Bob froze suddenly, sensing danger. The chimps slipped into the shadows and listened intently. *Clomp, clomp, clomp!* The odd noise grew louder.

Then Babe appeared under the streetlight. His hoofs clomped, then stopped.

"Hey, get out of the light!" Bob cautioned.

"Where's the f-f-food?" Babe asked.

"Shh!" Bob and Zootie hissed in unison.

"I'll do anything," Babe volunteered.

Bob looked around the deserted street and said, "Keep your voice down."

"Really—anything. I have to eat!" Babe whispered urgently.

Easy was skeptical. "You don't even have any hands. What can you do?"

"What can I do? I can—I can do *lots*," Babe babbled. It was hard to think over the noisy voices in his tummy.

The chimps moved on.

Clomp, clomp, clomp. Babe trotted after them. "Er...sheep! I can herd sheep!" he exclaimed.

Zootie shook her head. "Go home, sweetie. You're making a spectacle of yourself."

Then suddenly Bob had an idea. "Wait a momentum. Ya know what, honey? I'm thinking I might have some of those sheep for him to herd."

"You do?" Zootie was confused.

"Uh-huh. I'll show ya," Bob said.

Soon the animals had reached the convenience store two blocks south of the hotel. Neon signs buzzed brightly in the darkness.

Babe followed the chimps behind the store. Security bars and warning signs decorated a chain-link fence topped with gleaming razor wire.

Bob stretched open a small hole in the fence. "They're in there," he told Babe.

"What kind? Border Leicester or Scottish black-face?" Babe could handle either type of sheep. But a good shepherd likes to plan these things.

Bob replied, "Bull terrier and Doberman pinsch-er. Very exotic breeds."

Babe had never heard of those. But Rex had told him to do his best, whatever was asked of him. So the little pig started through the shadowy hole. Then he stopped and looked up. "Where do you want me to herd them?" he asked.

Bob answered, "That's up to you. Just keep them occupied till we get the necessaries."

"Okey-dokey!" Babe agreed. He wriggled through the fence.

The polite pig peered into the darkness and called, "Hello...hello? Anybody home?"

The answer was a long, low, spine-tingling snarl. Babe shuddered. "Um...anybody else?"

A creature of pure menace hulked out of the shadows. The Doberman spoke through clenched jaws. "You must have a thin grasp on reality. Unless you're suicidal," he said.

"I'm looking for some sheep," Babe explained.

If the Doberman's initial growl had been menac-ing, the sound that next issued from the darkness was totally terrifying.

The Doberman shrugged his muscular shoul-ders. "I warned ya..."

RAARGH! A beast whose every atom was dedicated to death and destruction came charging straight at Babe.

Just before he turned and ran, the little pig identified the blur of hatred as a bull terrier. This, of course, was not a sheep but a breed of dog known for its ferocity. Once the powerful jaws of a bull terrier closed on you...

Babe did not wait to find out if the horror stories were true. He bolted, and the beast's jaws snapped inches from his plump rump!

Snap! The bull terrier's chain yanked taut. Both dogs were chained to a stake in the ground.

Babe was already through the fence when he realized what had happened. He turned and poked his head back through the hole. "What's wrong with you? I was just trying to have a civil conversation."

The bull terrier strained at the chain with such fury that the stake started to pull out of the ground.

Oblivious to the danger, Babe continued. "Hasn't anyone ever taught you any manners?"

The bull terrier lunged. The stake popped out of the ground. Babe ran for his life. The bull terrier crashed through the fence, dragging the Doberman behind him.

Babe's little trotters skittered on the pavement. He wanted to run like the wind—or at least a race

Hoggett Hollow, where our story begins.

Farmer Hoggett, moments before the big accident.

Babe and the farmer's wife set off for the city.
The mice come along for the ride.

Babe meets his first city dweller.

The Flealands Hotel.

Some of the hotel's
many residents.

Babe takes in the view...

...while Tug steals Mrs. Hoggett's suitcase!

Babe meets the chimps: Bob, Zootie, and Easy.

The Doberman and the bull terrier chase after Babe.

Babe and his newest friend.

Raiders storm the hotel.

Babe uses his nose to find his missing friends.

Babe and Ferdinand find themselves
in the middle of a fancy banquet!

Mrs. Hoggett to the rescue!

The mice are happy to be home.

horse. But he was just a pig! With every step, the dogs loomed closer!

Babe squealed around the corner, doomed as a turkey at Thanksgiving. But the dogs were divided over whether to take the turn close or wide. They wound up on either side of a lamppost. Their chains looped around the streetlight's base and...*yank!*

Once again, fate had spared the small pig.

But the bull terrier refused to quit. He tugged so hard that the Doberman had to walk backward. The big dog pulled free of his collar. The bull terrier, dragging chain, stake, and his partner's empty collar, resumed his pursuit of the pig.

Babe ran madly for the sanctuary of the Flealands Hotel. He scratched at the door and squealed, "It's me. It's me. Please, somebody..."

Babe looked over his shoulder. The bull terrier's jaws hung open. Strands of slobber swung from the large, terrible teeth.

"Let me in!" Babe begged.

Thelonius, still slumped in the window, lifted his head. Tug listened.

Babe pleaded, *"Lettt meeee iiinn!"*

The bull terrier pounced! Babe scooted. Tug opened the door in time to see the crazed canine chase Babe around the corner. The little monkey quickly shut the door.

Directly across the canal, a suspicious neighbor opened her door and stared at the now-empty street. Her husband called from inside, "Darling, don't get yourself into a state."

"It's not my imagination. Something is going on in that house!" the woman stated with shrill conviction.

Her husband tried another approach. "Hortense, you're missing the aria."

Babe feared he was about to witness his own finale. Having narrowly escaped the bull terrier, the pig found himself snout-to-nose with the Doberman!

The pig veered wildly down an alley. He soon found himself in an ominous place. Sinister creatures stepped from the shadows. These dogs and cats scratched out a bitter living on the streets. They slept in discarded boxes clustered into a miserable metropolis known as Cardboard City.

Babe ran past them, turned, and saw a junkyard: a vast landscape of old TVs, conked-out computers, and other casualties of consumerism piled high in endless rows.

Babe bolted down one of the narrow alleys between the dunes of trash. The bull terrier followed him, but the Doberman ducked down a different alley, hoping to set up an ambush.

At the end of the lane, the dogs found each other,

but no pig! They stared in surprise. All they could hear was the sound of their own panting.

"Stop!" the bull terrier commanded.

"Stop what?!" the Doberman asked.

"Stop breathing!!" the bull terrier said crossly.

Both dogs held their breath. *Pant, pant, pant.* Someone was still panting!

The dogs looked up and saw the out-of-breath Babe perched on a box just inches above their heads.

Babe's trotters scrambled for footing on a pile of plastic pipes. The slippery tubes rolled down on the dogs. But that did not stop them!

Babe teetered precariously on the top of a mountain of clattering aluminum cans. With the same sickening certainty he'd felt when the tower in the kitchen tumbled, Babe knew he was going to fall.

KE-RASH! CLATTER! The cans sounded like metal surf smashing on steel rocks. The little pig slid out of control. He landed face first in one of the big plastic pipes! The sides were tight, but momentum took him toward the bottom.

Without a second's thought, the bull terrier dived in after Babe—and promptly got stuck! His stubby legs protruded from the bottom of the pipe; Babe's desperate head and frantic forelegs poked out of the top.

Homeless animals emerged from the shadows to gape at the amazing sight.

"Pig-dog! Pig-dog! Hot-diggety-blubbery-cat custard!" shouted one dog.

The bull terrier's flailing chain snagged on a stack of tires. The weight of the tires tugged the dog out of the pipe. Babe staggered on, still stuck.

Then the Doberman grabbed the other end of the pipe and shook it so hard that Babe popped free.

But at just that moment, the pile of tires collapsed, toppling everything in its path. Babe looked up to see himself about to be swept under a tidal wave of junk!

The pig tried to outrun the junk, but it was gaining on him! Two terrified cats, also similarly doomed, ducked through a small hole under the fence. Babe threw himself after them.

CRASH! The wave of junk smashed into the fence. Babe squeezed out on the other side, free!

But the persistent bull terrier and the deadly Doberman simply scaled the junk-pile wave to get back on Babe's trail.

The pig's little eyes scanned for any possible means of salvation. He shot through a gate propped open by a rusty lawnmower.

The bull terrier chased Babe across someone's yard. When the dog's chain hooked the lawnmower, he simply dragged the clanking machine after him.

Babe ran past a swing set, then splashed through a kiddy pool and into a teepee, which promptly collapsed on him. He thrashed blindly through a wall of bushes, scattering fragrant flowers everywhere.

Lights snapped on in a nearby house. A man in pajamas rushed out in time to see the bull terrier and the Doberman tearing apart a large doll.

"Mama! Mama!" the doll cried.

The man turned on the garden hose and blasted the dogs with cold water. The bull terrier turned on the man, who wisely ran inside. The hose jumped around like a mad serpent, spewing water.

The bull terrier looked around in frustration. The only target its small, dark eyes could see was the Doberman. He attacked!

"Hey! Ow! It's *me!*" the Doberman protested.

The bull terrier was beyond reason. "Massacre… slaughter," the mad dog mumbled.

"I'm your pal. Your *only* pal, doggone it…" the Doberman reasoned.

"…carnage…WAR!" The bull terrier ground his mighty teeth.

The Doberman ran!

The bull terrier's eyes had turned into pits of pure evil. His entire brain was given over to one terrible urge, leaving room for only a single word: *"Annihilation!"*

A walking teepee wandered into the park next door. The strange, ghostlike creature zigzagged past a

gazebo where three chimps were perched like gar-
goyles.

Their raid on the convenience store had not been
a complete failure. The chimps had grabbed a few
chocolates and a large jar of jellybeans.

Easy climbed down the gazebo and grabbed one
end of the teepee. The tarp lifted, and there was
Babe!

Just then, the bull terrier came thundering
toward them, still dragging the lawnmower. Easy
leaped back onto the gazebo. He looked down, wondering if he should help the hapless pig.

Easy shrugged at Bob. "Why get involved,
right?"

As the bull terrier closed in on his prey, Babe
tried to scramble up the gazebo. But there was no
way he could succeed. He had no choice but to run!

An audience of homeless animals gathered to
watch the pig try to outrun the relentless bull terrier.
Appropriately dramatic opera music blasted from the
suspicious neighbor's house, as the tragic hero's trotters brought him back to the bridge in front of the
hotel.

Thelonius stepped out onto the Flealands' balcony to watch as the bull terrier chased Babe over the
bridge. His terrible teeth scratched the pig's rump for
a first taste of blood!

But the lawnmower knocked over a newspaper

vending machine, which gave the pig a moment to contemplate his imminent destruction. Time slowed down for him. Each agonizing step, each searing breath brought a kind of horrible awareness.

Something broke through the terror—flickerings...fragments of his short life...the random events that had delivered him to this, his moment of annihilation.

The little pig simply could not go on.

As terror gave way to exhaustion and exhaustion to resignation, Babe turned to his attacker. His eyes filled with one simple question—Why?

There was no answer, only action. The bull terrier brought Babe down. A jumbo jet's loud flight drowned out our hero's squeals.

The spectators shuddered in the safety of the shadows. "Shouldn't somebody do something?" wondered a pink poodle with a faint Southern accent.

"Not our business," barked the itchy dog beside her.

The chimps watched from the gazebo. Nigel and Alan, along with other Flealands residents, peeked out from behind the hotel's faded curtains.

Nigel shook his large tan head. "That's what happens on the outside, Alan."

The mastiff added sadly, "It's the times, Nigel."

Flealick could not reach the window sill. His

checkered flag whipped back and forth. "What's hap-hap-happening?" he demanded.

Nigel could not bring himself to describe the horror. The bull terrier tossed Babe in the air as easily as he had the crying doll. But, as luck would have it, those terrible teeth did not pierce Babe's throat. They merely cut through his leather collar! The collar broke, and Babe went tumbling into the canal once again! *KER-SPLASH!*

Without hesitating, the bull terrier launched himself out over the sluggish water.

Dear ones, it is often said that he who lives by the sword dies by the sword. Anyone who dedicates his life to destruction will himself be destroyed.

So it was with the bull terrier. His launch into space was cut short by the lawnmower, still dragging in his wake. The mower hooked around the fallen newspaper vending machine. Once again, the chain pulled taut!

This time, the bull terrier found himself in a most unusual predicament. His hind legs were tangled in the chain. He was dangling upside down. The cold canal water flowed just inches below his nose. Did this dire circumstance diminish his desire for destruction? Did the dog regret the cruel chase?

No! The bound canine swung above the oil-scummed water, trussed up like a Sunday goose, still boiling with hatred. Since he could not see anyone else, he barked and strained at his own reflection in the brackish brine.

The chain slipped! The bull terrier's nose skimmed the cool water. Panic gripped his heart. The chase had turned on him: Now the killer was fighting for his life.

The bull terrier's struggles only caused the chain to slip further. The mower broke free of the vending machine and he dropped: still dangling, still tangled, but now with his head fully under the sluggish stream!

Babe shook himself dry. A short swim through the greasy water had brought him to the embankment in front of the hotel. The pig looked back to see…

The bull terrier was drowning!

Thelonius, Tug, the chimps, other Flealands residents, the homeless animals, and Babe all watched the bull terrier's powerful legs kick and thrash. The fetid water around his terrible snout churned.

He wanted to live! How could *he* be dying? But he was. The legs grew weaker. The great muscles, deprived of vital oxygen, could no longer move.

The sweet sounds of opera drifted over the still water.

The show was over. The homeless animals turned to go back to their cardboard shacks. Nigel and Alan stepped away from the window. Thelonius turned his broad back to the canal.

Then they all heard a splash.

Babe swam toward a small boat tethered nearby. He managed to free the boat and, dog-paddling like crazy, pushed the craft toward the bull terrier.

The show was *not* over. The animal audience returned. Thelonius stared in disbelief as Babe shoved the boat under his attacker. The chimps gasped as the dangling dog's body twitched with life, forelegs scrambling for a footing.

The homeless animals were amazed when the bull terrier pulled himself out of the water, choking, coughing, gulping up air. He was alive! But he was still tangled up in the chain.

The bystanders heard Babe cry, "Please! Someone! Give us a hand!"

A tiny monkey climbed down to the chain. Tug looked at Babe and shrugged. "Siht dnah ro taht dnah?" he asked. (*This hand or that hand?*)

The silly monkey giggled at his own joke, but quickly unhooked the bull terrier's chain from his collar. Babe made for the shore as the dog wriggled free of the chain.

Babe collapsed on the pavement. He was soon surrounded by homeless animals eager to make his acquaintance. The exhausted pig was a hero!

The pink poodle sidled up to him. Her once-glamorous curls were slightly matted. The proud poof of her tail had been fuzzed into scruffiness by the tangles of time. "Kind sir, kind sir. Can you help *me?*" she drawled. "I have been cruelly cast out and have nowhere to go."

"B-b-but how? What can I—" Babe stammered.

"Please, please. I know you're different from the others. Those that have had their way with me make their empty promises, but they're all lies...lies. I'm cold and afraid and terribly, terribly tired," she droned on.

"Um...where is your human?" Babe asked.

"She belongs to someone else now," she said. "Someone younger and prettier. Maybe it was my fault. Maybe if I'd tried harder..."

The pleas of the homeless filled Babe's ears.

"I—I—I never even h-h-had a hu-hu-human," stammered a dog with a persistent itch.

"I'm hungry," squeaked a starving kitten with a voice quieter than a mouse's.

And on it went. Creatures had been abandoned, dumped, and otherwise left to die. And they all thought that, somehow, Babe could solve their problems.

"Kind sir, you were sent here for a reason," the pink poodle asserted. "Take pity on us. We are the excluded and have nowhere to go."

"Well, it's nice and warm inside," Babe offered.

Bob stepped forward. "Not a good idea," the chimp said.

"But they—" Babe argued.

"No! No! Negatory! No-ness!" Bob shouted.

An old dog noticed the jar of jellybeans Bob carried. "Could that be food?" he barked.

The chimp clutched the jar to his chest.

"Oh, yum! Oh, yumyumyumyum!" The dog danced around excitedly, barking and scratching, scratching and barking.

"Have mercy. I'm faint with hunger," the pink poodle whined.

Bob backed away.

"Food. Food. Can't remember when I last ate. Any little tidbit. Just a lick. A sniff! Food! Food! Food!" the voices cried in a chorus of need.

"Quiet! Quiet!" Thelonius thundered from the balcony. The animals looked up. The old orangutan scanned the street, shaking his head with worry. "You'll bring all manner of trouble."

"Perhaps if we all went inside and lined up, I'm sure there'll be enough to go around," Babe suggested.

Bob said gruffly, "Hey, you're talking as if you're the word around here."

A low, dangerous voice growled, "I'd say he is."

"Who says?" Bob demanded.

A rumbling growl parted the crowd of homeless animals to leave the bull terrier standing alone. "I'd like to offer a solution that I feel confident you'll all respond to."

Bob was skeptical. "Oh?"

"Whatever the pig says, goes," the bull terrier declared.

A silence followed. No one dared to challenge those powerful jaws.

"Anyone hostile to the notion?" the bull terrier demanded.

Agreement poured forth from every available mouth. "Absolutely not! Whatever he says. You got it!"

"Anybody else?" the bull terrier asked.

Bob had not liked the look of the bull terrier's teeth from a distance, but up close... "Fine by *moi*," he said.

"Anybody else?" the bull terrier asked again.

All eyes turned to Thelonius. The aged ape shrugged. "It's still just a pig."

Like the animals seeking shelter on Noah's Ark, the homeless filed inside the Flealands Hotel. The pink poodle surveyed her surroundings. To the down-and-out dog, the shabby hotel looked like luxury.

"Oh, my!" she exclaimed. "This recalls the glory

days of my youth when I was dizzy with privilege. I had my hair styled and my nails manicured."

The Flealands' resident population regarded the visitors with suspicion. From the landing of the dog floor, Nigel sniffed. "Riffraff with no manners. They'll soil willy-nilly, won't they, Alan?"

The mastiff's heavy black head nodded. "Willy-nilly, Nigel."

Babe watched the last of the homeless animals enter the hotel. Then he heard a gruff voice say, "Hey, swine…I want you to have this."

Babe turned and saw the bull terrier. Tug had unbuckled the dog's spiked leather collar. Its sharp points shone like metal teeth in the little monkey's outstretched paw.

"Um…that's not necessary," the pig said.

"Yes it is," the bull terrier insisted.

Babe did not want the mean-looking thing. "You're very kind, but…"

"Oh, I'm anything but kind. In fact, I have a professional obligation to be malicious," the bull terrier confessed.

"Then you should change jobs," Babe suggested.

"I can't," the dog declared.

The pig disagreed. "Yes, you can."

The bull terrier shrugged. "It's in the bloodline, you see. We were once warriors. Now there's just the urge…"

Babe shook his head. "That's no excuse."

The bull terrier looked sad. "A murderous shadow lies hard across my soul."

Babe was not sure he understood. "So…should I have let you drown?"

"Most would have." The bull terrier was still deeply confused by Babe's actions. "Pig, if you were to wear my collar, it would honor me."

Inside the Flealands Hotel, a curious ritual was being repeated many times.

"Thank the pig," recited the bull terrier as each animal reached the front of a long, orderly line looping through the hotel.

"Thank you, pig," each animal said while accepting a ration of jellybeans from Tug.

"You're welcome," Babe replied.

Babe felt embarrassed when the chimps took their turn. "Thank you, little thingy," Zootie said.

But Bob just took his beans.

"Come again?" the bull terrier said.

Babe whispered to the dog. "It's okay. Really."

But the bull terrier was not about to let the matter rest. "Hey, *you!*" he barked to Bob.

The chimp whispered resentfully, "Thanks."

"Don't mention it," Babe replied eagerly. "You're awfully welcome."

Easy accepted his beans and nodded shyly at

Babe. "Thank you…y-y-y' honor."

In Uncle Fugly's deserted digs, Thelonius listened glumly and dropped the last flake of food into the fishbowl. The feisty little swimmer was still hungry—and so were all the other animals in the Flealands Hotel!

Indeed, dear ones, there was more than a little sniping and griping accompanying the belly rumbles. "I'm still hungry," complained the little kitten.

The itchy dog scratched and moaned. "Coupla jellybeans don't even hit the bottom."

"If only there weren't so many of those cats!" Nigel sniffed.

To which some cats naturally took offense. Babe's attempts to stop the fight failed until the bull terrier shouted, "Hey! The pig has something to say."

"Um…er…cats and dogs should be nicer to each other," Babe said.

"Right, the chief has spoken," the bull terrier concluded. "It is decreed that all cats and dogs shall henceforth put aside their instinctive and fanatical abhorrence of each other."

Babe hadn't realized he'd said all that! "Thank you," he said.

But the bull terrier was on a roll. "And that hereafter all creatures great and diminutive shall be of equal stature with rights to liberty and justice that nobody can deny, and so say all of us."

In the stunned silence that followed, the little kitten mewed, "I'm still hungry."

Then Zootie said, "My tummy feels all... thingy."

"I know, honey," Bob agreed. "We did all the work. We shoulda got the most."

Zootie moaned! She put her hand on her swollen belly. "It hurts here," the pregnant chimp said.

Bob put his ear to his wife's belly and listened.

"What? What's wrong?!" Easy demanded.

Bob smiled. "Nothing."

And so, dear ones, this topsy-turvy night was to end with a beginning...

Chapter Seven

Sanctuary's End

This event, which weaves a thread from past to future, soothed the tired hearts of those assembled, and for a while, at least, they put aside their uncertainties.

Something wonderful wiggled in Zootie's arms. Easy saw two tiny, fuzzy heads and four teeny flappy ears. One of the two minuscule noses let out a little sneeze.

"I'm an uncle." Easy's eyes were wide with awe.

"Twice," said Bob, who could not stop staring at the double bundle.

Bob and Easy high-fived. Animals who did not have five fingers expressed their congratulations in other ways.

"Well, bite my tail!" one dog enthused.

"They've got their father's ears!" cooed another.

Thelonius watched but said nothing. The bull terrier, on the other paw, addressed the assembly grandly, "On behalf of us all, I'm sure the chief would like to extend a special welcome. So *listen up!*"

Babe did not know what to say that could possibly express the awesome joy of the occasion. So he sang. "La, la, la. La, la, la…"

The bull terrier joined in, followed by the hungry little kitten, then the itchy dog, until soon the entire Flealands feline chorus and all the other animals, homeless and resident alike, were singing with full-throated, merry abandon.

La, laaaaaa!

"Shh!" Thelonius cautioned. But even the feisty fish had joined in the song.

La, la, la, laaaaa!

The sound traveled over the canal, between the stone canyons of skyscrapers, to the arms of an angel on top of a church. Ferdinand lifted his head. His feathers prickled with excitement. The duck knew that song. His lucky pig sang that song! Babe was near! The fowl flew off to follow the tune.

Unfortunately, Ferdinand was not the only one to hear the spontaneous meowing, woofing, and howling ode to joy. The suspicious neighbor shrilled, "My God, Roger! The place is teeming! Overrun with filthy animals!"

Babe threw back his head to sing even louder and

spotted a familiar face at the tower window. Ferdinand tapped his beak against the glass. Babe scrambled up the stairs, followed by the bull terrier.

As soon as the pig threw open the window, Ferdinand flew at him. "Give us a peck. C'mon, pig. Kisskisskisskiss!" The duck looked around the room. "Who are these losers?" Then he saw the bull terrier. "Who's this?"

"I'm his conflict resolution consultant," the bull terrier explained.

Ferdinand blinked at the spiked collar around Babe's neck. "What's goin' on here? You look...different."

"Yeah, well, this place can really take it outta ya." Babe sighed. So much had happened since leaving the farm!

"Tell me about it," Ferdinand agreed. "But, hey, I'm with my pig, my lucky, lucky pig. Li' ol' Ferdie. Snug and safe at last!"

Just then, *CRASH!* A gloved hand smashed through the glass panel in the front door. In seconds, the hotel was being stormed by a band of raiders. These bullies had disguised themselves with badges and justified themselves with papers filled with fine print. But their actions soon showed their true colors.

One was a doctor. She wore a starched white lab coat over her flowered dress. "Check upstairs," she told a muscular motorcycle cop.

One man wearing protective padding bent to stroke a cat who leaned against him lovingly.

The man's partner offered food pellets to the pink poodle. "Ooh, well, bite my tail," she cooed. The poodle pranced on her hind legs for the tall, gangly man, then rolled on her back.

"Doll, be careful," the bull terrier muttered under his breath. The bully knew a bully when he saw one. But the pink poodle was a fool for food. Tail wagging, she allowed herself to be led out the door.

"No one home!" the motorcycle cop called from upstairs.

One of the raiders stuck up a NOTICE OF IMPOUNDMENT on the front door.

Ferdinand panicked! "Feet! Feet! Time to retreat!" The frantic fowl ran straight into the motorcycle cop, who grabbed him by the neck.

The cruel cop chuckled. "Hey...supper!"

Babe was not a violent pig. But in defense of his friend, he did his best bull terrier imitation. *"Rarrrgh!"* Babe charged the leather-clad cop.

The cop laughed, easily snatching up the defenseless pig. "Yo...breakfast!"

But the laugh was short-lived. Because this time a real bull terrier came bounding at him! The cop reached for his gun, but the dog was already snapping at his throat!

Another of the raiders ran to his rescue. The huge, padded man leaped over the pig and started pounding on the bull terrier with his truncheon.

Cats and dogs poured out of the hotel from every possible exit, scattering over the rooftops and into the streets. Some reached freedom. Others were snatched back as they made their break.

The motorcycle cop rubbed his neck as he came down the stairs. He was glad to see the big raider dragging away his attacker. The bull terrier's savage snout was restrained by a metal muzzle bristling with buckles and a shiny steel lock.

Babe watched helplessly. Behind him a lampshade trembled. Feathers decorated the lamp's peculiar base, which consisted of a pair of shivering duck legs.

The animals could do nothing against this troop of humans armed with tranquilizer guns, darts, and nets. Though Bob tried desperately to defend his babies, he soon succumbed to several darts.

Zootie looked up at Thelonius and begged, "Please, Thelonius! Do something!"

The orangutan turned away. On his way back to Fugly's apartment, Thelonius passed Babe. He stared into those twinkly little pig eyes and spat, "You did this!"

Easy, Zootie, and the twins were cruelly captured. Then another of the raiders threw open the door of Fugly's room. "Get a load of this!" he called to his companions.

The other invaders peered through the door to see Thelonius standing in the center of the room. The orangutan held Fugly's blanket, a small suitcase, and the fishbowl. He looked like the perfect English butler, packed and ready for a trip.

Babe watched the raiders advance on Thelonius. "Careful," an invader cautioned. "They're incredibly strong."

One of them slinked behind the beast. At a nod, they all rushed. One of them threw a net over Thelonius. In the process, he bumped the fishbowl, which smashed on the floor.

As the men dragged Thelonius away, the feisty fish flapped in a sparkling puddle between shards of broken glass.

"Mercy…mercy…" he gasped.

Babe hurried to the desperate fish. As he tried to figure out what to do, a noose dropped around Babe's neck!

The raider was already loaded down with several cats, but the big padded man dragged Babe behind him by the noose. The pig glanced back to see the poor fish still flapping on the floor.

The miserable prisoners formed a sad parade down the steps of the Flealands Hotel. In the landlady's apartment, a few animals still enjoyed their freedom, but not for long.

"Ah-ah-choo!" Ferdinand sneezed. "Are there any cats in here?" he asked in a nasal voice.

"Cats? No way!" Flealick snapped. "No cat would dare come in here!"

"But I'm allergic to ca-ca-AH-AH-CHOO!" Ferdinand's words turned into a violent sneeze. "I'm telling you, there are *cats* in here."

In his haste to rid the room of that hated species, Flealick forgot who the real enemy was.

As he passed the landlady's door, the motorcycle cop heard the muffled barks and yeowls of a cat and dog fight. The officer marched inside and lifted the bed. A duck, a dog on wheels, and a dozen cats froze in shock on a battlefield littered with fur and feathers.

With a skitter of claws, the creatures scattered. Ferdinand shot out between the cop's black leather boots.

Flealick scooted for the door, then felt his wheels leave the ground. He struggled, but he was no match for the motorcycle cop!

Nigel and Alan crept out of their hiding place in the closet. The big dogs looked around in panic.

"Flealick! Flealick!" the bulldog called.

His huge mastiff companion shook like a chihuahua in a blizzard. "Flealick's gone, Nigel!" Alan barked. Everything that was safety, home, comfort, and companionship was suddenly gone!

Ferdinand was intent on making his escape. Unfortunately, as he cleared the corner of the second floor landing, he ran right into a raider's legs. Webbed orange feet squeaked on the floor as he made an abrupt course change. Ferdinand launched himself through the railings of the banister toward the ground floor.

The duck landed right on another raider's head! The big guy dragging Babe was so startled that he bumped into a bookcase—*THUD!* The bookcase crashed into a table—*THUMP!*—and knocked over a vase—*CRASH!*—and a potted plant—*CRACK!*

In the confusion, Babe broke free. The handle of the noose thumped on the stairs behind him as he raced up to Fugly's apartment.

Babe skidded across the floor to the puddle and quickly slurped up the still-flapping fish. The three mice did not understand what the pig was up to. Sure he was hungry, but this was hardly the time...

Babe ran to the open kitchen window, took careful aim, and *THWOO!*—spit the fish out and into the canal...*PLOP!*

The fish breathed in the cool water all around him. He flapped his fins and wiggled his tail. He did not mind the bits of gum wrapper or the occasional bottle cap. He was free at last! Yes, dear ones, he was alive, swimming, and free at last!

Tug gave Babe the thumbs-up sign. But the pig had no time to feel proud for having saved the fish. The big raider thundered into the room!

Babe's eyes darted for some means of escape. The answer came to him: Follow the fish! The pig clambered up to the window. He dived toward the canal, but the raider lunged after him. The big man's hands managed to snag Babe's collar. Babe dangled over the sidewalk.

Then the raider jumped! Something had pinched his bottom! The big guy tumbled out the window and into the canal!

Tug laughed. Dear ones, perhaps you've already guessed whose little hands had tweaked that big bottom.

In the alley behind the hotel, a van was parked behind a police car and a police motorcycle. Nigel and Alan watched the invaders load their live loot into cages inside the van. Nigel spotted Flealick's checkered flag as a raider handed the little dog to a human inside the van.

The big dogs did not know what to do! Could they possibly hope to overcome so many humans? Perhaps there would be a chance for escape later. Whatever happened, they could not abandon Flealick! Who would make sure he didn't roll too fast? Who would remind him to take his medicine and lick behind his ears? The loyal friends exchanged a look, then leaped into the back of the van.

At that moment, a voice inside the van grumbled, "This one's useless. Look at him."

Rough hands tossed the crippled dog out of the van. Meanwhile, other hands slammed the doors shut. Nigel and Alan were trapped inside!

Flealick went wild! The little dog snapped at the nearest ankles, which happened to belong to the doctor. She snatched up her lab coat and kicked at Flealick.

The raider who'd gone after Babe dripped out of the shadows. The padding that had protected him from the bull terrier squished with each step as he angrily made his way to the official car.

"Don't even ask!" he told his partner.

His gangly companion shrugged. It had been a strange shift. Even in the big city you didn't see orangutans in butler suits every night!

From the safety of the shadows, a wet pig and a small monkey watched the vehicles depart. The doctor had not been entirely successful in kicking away Flealick. In fact, because the persistent pooch was still tugging at her hem, the doctor slammed her dress in the van's door.

Flealick clung to that strip of flowered cloth— and would not let go!

Babe stepped out of the shadows. What was Flealick doing? The little dog would get himself killed!

"Flealick, let go!" Babe shouted. *"Let go!"*

Babe turned to Tug. The two started chasing the van.

On the Flealands' roof, Ferdinand freaked. "Pig. Pig. Whaddaya doing to me?"

The duck did not care what happened to the little dog or any of the other strange creatures he had met at the hotel. But Ferdinand could not lose his lucky pig.

Flealick was fortunate he did not get run over. The van swerved. The dog's wheels burned rubber! The dress ripped just a little more with each curve. Every second flung Flealick closer to the van's massive back wheels!

Babe and Tug could not keep up with the speeding vehicles. They trotted breathlessly after the convoy, fearing greatly for the fate of their senseless friend. Yes, dear ones, you may recall that Flealick's sense of smell was poor, his eyesight failing, and as for hitching a ride on a speeding hem, well, that certainly rates as risky, if not downright senseless.

But perhaps because the dog's intentions were noble, or because the doctor did not buy the best dresses, before the tires could crush the canine's cranium, the van turned a corner—and the hem ripped!

Flealick hurtled across the deserted main road. *TUMBLE—CRASH—BANG!* The little dog bounced head-over-wheels into an empty side street.

Babe's collar clattered as he turned the corner and saw a most horrible sight.

The crippled dog lay flat on his back in the gutter. One unsteady wheel spun slowly, but otherwise, the frail figure lay perfectly still.

Babe feared the worst. "Flealick? Flealick?" The pig licked the dog's snout. One red eye opened. Babe tried again, "Can you hear me?"

Flealick's dazed reply was muffled by a slobbery wad of flowered cloth.

"Huh?" Babe asked.

Tug removed the cloth.

"Don't worry," Flealick said faintly. "I got their scent. Flip me over."

Babe was worried. "Are you okay?"

"Yeah, yeah. Hurry. Hurry!" Flealick barked impatiently.

Tug and Babe pulled Flealick upright. The little dog shook his head, trying to clear it. "Feelin' good. Feelin' peppy!" he said.

Flealick snuffled the air. "They went this-a-way," he declared, pointing his clogged nose back toward the hotel.

Babe inhaled deeply. "Actually, Flealick...I think it's *that* way."

Ferdinand flapped his wings hysterically. "Wait a minute. Whaddaya doing?"

Babe felt proud. "It's all in the hooter, Ferdie, the schnoz." The beagle at the airport had been right. Babe *did* have a good nose. And the time had come for him to use it!

"The *what?*" Ferdinand demanded.

"The olfactory instrument," Babe explained calmly.

The duck became even more hysterical. "Pig. Pig, you're unraveling here. Pull yourself together and listen to reason. (a) They're long gone. (b) They were not nice people. (c) is for kamikaze. And (d) is for delusional, which is what you are in the head!"

Dear ones, you probably noticed that C is not the first letter in the word *kamikaze*. You may also recall what the old sheepdog, Rex, told Babe about listening to the duck. Babe remembered the wise dog saying, "Don't take counsel of your fears."

"Ferdie," Babe began.

Ferdinand fumed. "Face it. You're just a little pig in the big city! What can you possibly do?! What can *anyone* do? WHY EVEN TRY?"

Babe wondered if the duck was right. Maybe one little pig could not make a difference. Maybe he couldn't even save his own neck, much less anyone else's.

Then the pig heard something squeak. He turned and saw a crippled, half-blind dog with no sense of smell rolling his dented harness down the street to save his friends.

Babe considered his options. Then he turned to Tug. "Would you help me off with this, please?"

Tug lifted the noose over Babe's pinkish head. The pig trotted after Flealick.

The duck sighed as he followed his friend. "Ferdinand the duck. Witness to insanity."

Chapter Eight

Where Do We Belong?

Sometimes we discover our talents only through necessity. Babe, who had never used his nose for anything but the pursuit of food, soon found he could make his way through the trickiest of smellscapes.

The rich, chocolaty aroma of freshly ground coffee drifted toward his nostrils, blending with sweet bakery smells and the salty odor of a fish market. Each alley, each passing truck, each perfumed pedestrian brought new scents for Babe's sensitive schnoz. The sights and sounds of the city, its gleaming towers and rushing rivers of traffic, faded as the pig focused on that single sense.

Eventually, Babe felt so in tune with his hooter that he half believed it was talking to him. His snout wasn't as loud as his belly had been, but its small voice was quite clear. Finally, the pig's pink proboscis stated, "I do believe we're here."

And sure enough, when the animals turned the next corner...

"*Ta-daaa!*" Babe's snout crowed triumphantly.

The raiders' van was parked outside a building in the University Hospital complex.

Babe's nose led the four friends to a window in one of the large, modern buildings. Lights flashed.

While Ferdinand, Flealick, and Babe hid in some bushes, Tug climbed up a drainpipe and peeked inside. A photographer was snapping mug shots of the Flealands' residents. Thelonius stood against a measuring board. His clothes had been removed. The chimps, also undressed, and the other animals watched from their cages.

FLASH! The human photographed Thelonius's left profile. He pushed the ape's chin the other way.

FLASH! The photographer snapped Thelonius's right profile. Then he turned his flashing machine on the newborn chimps.

Tug looked into another window and saw another horror: Rows and rows of rabbits poked their heads out of metal boxes.

Tug scrambled to join Babe, Flealick, and Ferdinand. The little monkey gestured wildly and gibbered hysterically.

"Let's go get 'em!" Flealick started rolling out of

the bushes, but Babe stuck a trotter between the spokes of the dog's wheels.

At that moment, two humans in lab coats strolled past the animals. The four friends held their breath.

When the people had passed, Babe cautioned, "If we get caught, we won't be able to help anybody."

Esme Cordelia Hoggett also was trapped in an extremely difficult position. Dear ones, you can't already have forgotten the disaster that befell the poor farmer's wife when she went looking for Babe?

Covered in glue from head to toe, Mrs. Hoggett had been arrested, interrogated, examined, and forced to sleep in a windowless cell with a snoring criminal. Yet none of this pained her as much as knowing that she had failed in her mission.

But at last the farmer's wife had her day in court. In a wood-paneled room dedicated to justice, Mrs. Hoggett explained her view of things. "I've given myself a good hard talking to. I said, 'Esme, you've let Arthur down. You've let yourself down. And you've let the pig down. What are you, Esme Hoggett, if you can't look after a helpless creature that has been placed in your care and trusts you?'"

She looked at the judge. "Sir, I put to you a simple question. What is the worth of a pig? As a general rule, I used to dismiss pigs. But a pig became my husband's best friend. And I have to confess that made me a little jealous. But not anymore. So go ahead. Lock me in jail! Bind me in chains! The minute I am free, I shall march straight back into the streets and continue my search!"

The judge had never heard anyone speak so many words in so short a time. Evidently, this was a woman of clear conscience and good intent. Besides, the judge had grown up on a farm with many pink pals. The twinkling eyes in his round, pink face showed the judge had a fondness for pigs…but that's another story.

The judge pounded his gavel. "Case dismissed!"

Thanks to the cautious pig, the animals were able to gain access to the research building. They waited until most of the staff had left, then crept to the room where their friends were being kept.

After Tug's tiny paw turned the door handle, Babe looked into the dark room.

"Hello?" the pig called.

"It's the pinkness!" Bob exclaimed.

"It's the thingy!" Zootie added.

The bull terrier barked, "Chief!"

The pink poodle sighed. "I knew he'd come."

"Shh!" Babe whispered. "We have to be quiet."

But the animals were excited. Tug quickly set the chimps free. Together, they released the cats and dogs from their cages.

The bull terrier managed to speak around his muzzle. "Chief, I'm proud of ya."

The other animals surrounded Babe, eager to express their gratitude.

From his hiding place under the stairwell, Flealick watched two technicians load a cage onto a truck.

"I'll just lock up," one of them said.

Flealick panicked as he watched the technician head back into the building.

Meanwhile, Ferdinand was trying to save his feathers. "Okay, okay," he said. "You all know the term 'Survival of the Fastest'? Well, I got an idea. We split into two groups. The fast ones come with me. The slow ones stay behind and sacrifice themselves."

"Ferdinand!" Babe protested.

"Well, that way we don't *all* die," the duck explained. "I think that's only reasonable, don't you?"

Babe turned to the group. "May I suggest we stay calm, maintain a tight formation, and proceed in an orderly fashion."

Ferdinand panicked. "And may he suggest we do it real fast!"

"Where's Thelonius?" Easy asked.

The orangutan was in the corner, putting on his shirt.

"Whaddaya doing?" Bob asked him.

"I—I'm not dressed," Thelonius stated.

Babe said gently, "Mr. Thelonius. Time to go."

"But...I'm not...dressed," he protested.

Zootie said, "Thelonius, you're an oranguthingy."

The ape did not know what to do. In truth, dear ones, Thelonius did not even know what he was. Was he an oranguthingy or a human? A butler, a performer, or an ape? He stood frozen with indecision.

A clock ticked on the wall.

In the stairwell, Flealick cursed his wheels. He watched helplessly as the returning technician neared the top of the stairs.

Suddenly, the animals in the room heard footsteps.

"Quiet! Quiet!" Nigel woofed softly.

"Shush!" Alan added.

They scattered into the darkest corners of the room. Easy pulled Thelonius with him. They all held their breath.

The technician opened the door, glanced inside, rubbed his eyes, and yawned. Then he pulled the door shut and locked it behind him. When they heard the steps recede, the animals breathed again. Thelonius slowly put on his coat.

*   *   *

Just as one door closed, another one across town opened. Mrs. Hoggett entered the Flealands Hotel and was shocked by the wreckage. She picked her way over the broken glass from the front door and glanced up at the NOTICE OF IMPOUNDMENT.

On her way upstairs, she saw the broken vase and the potted plant that Ferdinand had tipped over when he startled one of the raiders. Water from the vase had mixed with dirt from the plant.

Mrs. Hoggett stopped in her tracks. There were footprints in the mud. She bent down to get a closer look. Her glue-starched dress split with a loud *riiiippp!*

Mrs. Hoggett didn't care. The tracks had definitely been made by the trotters of a pig.

"Pig?" Mrs. Hoggett called. "Pig? Pig, pig, pig!"

The farmer's wife followed the trail into Uncle Fugly's living room. The landlady was slumped in a chair by the window.

"Is the pig here?" Mrs. Hoggett asked.

"Gone," the landlady said. Her lips barely moved. Her chest hardly lifted with breath. Her eyes looked dull and lifeless.

"But he *was* here?" the farmer's wife persisted.

"They've all gone," the landlady reported in a hollow voice. "Every last one of them."

Mrs. Hoggett shook her head. "What happened, dear?"

The landlady's head sagged even lower. "This used to be such a lovely neighborhood. People caring, keeping an eye out for each other. They really did. What's the world coming to? I'm away one night, just one night, with my Uncle Fugly on his deathbed!"

The landlady burst into tears.

The farmer's wife hugged the stranger. The landlady's ear mashed against Mrs. Hoggett's glue-hardened dress.

The landlady poured out her pain. "It's all my fault. I thought I could make a true place, a kind place where they could be okay. But how can you do that here? It was stupid for me to even try. And now…Fugly's gone, but…but I wasn't *so* stupid, was I? Because we have to belong somewhere, don't we?"

Mrs. Hoggett patted the landlady's back. "Dear, who did this?" she asked gently.

"What did the animals ever do to her?" the landlady wondered.

"Who?" asked the farmer's wife.

"Her! That—" Anger gave the landlady new life. She pointed across the canal and shouted, *"Her!"*

Mrs. Hoggett leaped to her feet, and her dress broke! Slabs of glued fabric crashed to the floor.

"Right!" Mrs. Hoggett said. "Clothes! Got anything that will fit me?"

In a few moments, Mrs. Hoggett came charging out of the Flealands Hotel dressed in Fugly Floom's clown suit! She was dragging the landlady behind her.

Imagine the opera-loving, animal-hating neighbor's surprise on being roused from a sound sleep by the farmer's wife dressed as a clown! When the woman answered the door, Mrs. Hoggett screamed: *"We want our animals!"*

At that moment, those animals were making their way up a teetering tower of cages, boxes, stools, and chairs leading to a hole in the ceiling of the research building. Unlike the tower Babe had climbed in Uncle Fugly's kitchen, this was no cruel prank. Shaky though it was, the tower was the only way for the Flealands animals and their homeless companions to escape.

Once the tower was negotiated, the animals had to cross an air-conditioning pipe connecting the research lab to another hospital building. The pig led the way.

Toward the front of the line, the itchy dog scratched himself nervously. "So where are we going?" he asked.

The pink poodle didn't know. "Does it matter?

In this whole wide world is there anywhere that's truly, really safe?"

"Yeah, for my babies?" Zootie asked. The little twins had already been through so much in their short lives.

"Well, there is a place I know where everyone is inclined to be fair and good to each other," Babe said thoughtfully. "But it's ever so far away, and I'm not even sure it's there anymore."

In this place of steel pipes and steelier hearts, the little pig struggled to recall the green hills and warm hearts of home. He thought of a bandaged hand reaching out to scratch his head, and a certain soft voice that had once uttered the words, "That'll do, Pig. That'll do."

"I think he's talking about the 'fun,'" Easy explained to Zootie.

All of the animals had crossed the pipe except Nigel and Flealick. Flealick, because of his wheels, had remained on the ground floor. But Nigel...

The bulldog looked down at the ground far below him. "Alan! Alan!" he called. The bulldog's sturdy legs were frozen in fear.

Babe recognized a situation that called for firmness, as occasionally happened with the sheep back home. "Nigel. Get your big bottom over here," the pig said.

Nigel tried to get a grip. "I'm making a fool of

myself, aren't I, Alan? I'm absolutely rigid with anxiety, aren't I? I can't do it, can I, Alan?"

For the first time in their long friendship, the mastiff disagreed. "Yes, you *can,* Nigel!"

Through his muzzle, the bull terrier said, "Nige, you're a big brave wolf, bred for battle against the brute, the beast, the bear, and the bull!"

The bulldog shook his massive tan head. "I'm not a wolf. I'm just a big, fat scaredy-cat!"

The hungry little kitten spoke up. "That's it," he said. "Think cat. Pretend you're a cat." The tiny kitten, like all the other felines, had crossed the narrow bridge with complete confidence.

Babe saw the wisdom in the little cat's strategy. "Yes, Nigel. You're a cat!"

The ugly, musclebound dog repeated dutifully, "I'm a cat. I'm a very graceful..." He stretched one paw daintily onto the pipe. "...Svelte..." Nigel took another step into the void. "...Sure-footed pussycat."

The bulldog took two more steps, then panicked. "What if I fall?!"

For a moment, no one said a word. Then Ferdinand piped up, "Pretend you're a birdy."

Babe shot the duck a look.

"You're a cat! A custard-pipe, pig-dog, dog-cat," the stuttering dog exclaimed.

"I'm a cat," Nigel repeated. "I'm a cat. I'm a cat.

I'm a cat…" Slowly, the bulldog inched his way across the rest of the pipe.

The entire assembly sighed with relief as Nigel and Alan were reunited.

"Yeah," said the bull terrier. "Now, wasn't that great for your self-esteem?"

Nigel turned to the mastiff. "It was, wasn't it, Alan?"

The big black dog was glad to be in agreement once more. "Darn tootin', Nigel!"

The pink poodle gazed dreamily at the bull terrier. "Would you like to work on my self-esteem?" she asked the big dog.

Only one little boy was awake when the escapees entered the darkened Children's Ward. The sick child was the sole witness to a moonlit parade led by a pig. Chimpanzees, dogs, cats, and a duck made their way quietly past the sleeping patients toward the elevator that would take them down to freedom.

The little boy's jaw dropped in wonder when the last animal stopped and stared right at him! Though he loved animals and was always reading about them in books, the youngster had never seen an orangutan. The sad truth is, dear ones, that the boy had not seen much beyond the inside of doctors' offices. But on that magical night, by the glow of the moon, the delighted child saw an orangutan in a butler's uniform. Pain, fear, and illness were forgotten. The boy smiled!

If he had looked out the window at that moment, the child would have seen something even more amazing. The resourceful farmer's wife and the animal-loving landlady had employed the only means of transportation at hand: Uncle Fugly's trick tandem bicycle!

Exhausted from pedaling through traffic, the women had finally hitched a ride on the back of an ambulance. With each turn of the trick bicycle's wheels, the riders bounced up and down like demented pistons.

The brightly colored van screamed into the hospital complex, tandem in tow. The women bounced past various buildings, including one abuzz with activity. Sleek limousines gleamed under strands of fairy lights, opening their doors to women in glittering gowns and men in shiny top hats.

Suddenly, Mrs. Hoggett saw the sign she was looking for: RESEARCH LABORATORY. She let go of the ambulance, and the bike veered off.

As the bouncing ladies passed underneath the air-conditioning pipe, a little dog rolled out of the shadows barking frantically.

While Mrs. Hoggett and the landlady followed

Flealick, the little boy trailed the animal parade. He padded to the elevator at the end of the hall and pounded on the door.

The night nurse walked up. "Gosh, little man. What are you doing here?" she asked him.

The little boy pointed at the elevator and said, "Duck."

The nurse had never heard such nonsense in her life. She scooped up the child in her arms and took him back to bed.

The boy, of course, was right. There was a duck in the elevator, as well as an orangutan, several chimps, cats, dogs, one tiny monkey, and a pig, all on their way to the ground floor—and freedom!

The elevator doors whirred open again. A doctor chatting with a couple in evening dress did not notice the elevator doors open behind him. The group of escapees held their breaths!

But the man continued chatting, intent on his fund raising. The doors glided shut. The escapees breathed again and descended to the next floor.

Flealick had never been particularly good at finding things. He had led Mrs. Hoggett and the landlady to a dead end!

In the quiet alleyway, the women saw a kitchen helper drinking coffee.

"'Evening," he said.

"We're looking for some…er…animals," Mrs. Hoggett said.

"What kind?"

"Pig. Cats. Dogs. Monkeys…that sort of thing." The man just stared. "Uh-uh."

At that moment, the elevator reached its destination. The doors opened on a kitchen where a busy chef balanced an armload of pots and pans. The chef was a large red-faced man with a hot temper. He saw the animals, screamed, and dropped the pots with a loud crash.

Outside, Mrs. Hoggett and the landlady heard the sound of clattering pots, men shouting, dogs barking, and…a pig squealing.

Flealick shot through the helper's legs. Mrs. Hoggett and the landlady nearly knocked the man down in their haste to enter the kitchen.

Chefs and waiters chased the creatures around the crowded kitchen, but the animals fled through another door.

Mrs. Hoggett's chubby legs pumped faster than anyone would have thought possible. She had almost caught up with the animals when the chef grabbed her trick suspenders.

"Pig! Pig!" cried Mrs. Hoggett.

As he ran through the door, Babe glanced over

his shoulder and saw a vision: The boss's wife running toward him in a bright costume. Her suspenders stretched and stretched until her fingers
almost touched Babe's bristly white fur.

Then suddenly, she shot backward! The trick suspenders had reached their limit—and *SNAP!* Mrs.
Hoggett was back in the kitchen! The door slammed
shut. The vision was gone. But Babe's faith was
restored. The boss's wife was here! The farm was real.
There was hope!

"It's Her!" Babe squealed joyfully.

Thelonius was similarly moved by the round figure in the bright clown costume. "Himself," the
awestruck ape said to Easy. "I thought I saw...
Himself."

"Ferdie! The boss's wife. She's here!" Babe
exclaimed.

But the duck wasn't listening. "Er, Pig? Can I
borrow you for a moment?" he said.

Babe turned and for the first time saw where they
were. They had run from the kitchen straight into a
gigantic ballroom! Surrounding the linen-topped
tables, seated on gilded velvet chairs were the city's
wealthiest citizens wearing jewels, satin gowns, and
elegant black tuxedos.

"Well, bite my tail!" the pink poodle declared
with pleasure.

"This must be the 'fun,'" Easy said.

To one side was a mountain of food. Chefs in crisp white uniforms stood proudly beside their masterpieces.

Beyond them, a nervous waiter perched on a tall ladder beside his carefully constructed pyramid of champagne glasses.

The room was deadly quiet as the banquet guests stared at the animals.

Onstage, the grand matriarch held a huge cardboard check. Her hands were frozen in the act of presenting the check to a man in a tuxedo.

Hoping the animals were just part of the entertainment, she finally said, "Oh…what a surprise. I adore surprises."

Back on the dance floor, chefs, waiters, and a few helpful guests slowly advanced on the animals, trying to shoo them back into the kitchen.

But Ferdinand did not want to return to that room full of cleavers and sauces! The duck bolted for the tables. The others followed his lead, scattering in all directions.

Babe ran toward a group of ladies and hid in the billowing folds of their flowing gowns, with Ferdinand right behind him.

Bob's only thought was for the safety of his children. With Zootie clutching the twins, he cleared a path to the mezzanine. The chimp hoped that the upper level would be safe from the shrieking, flailing humans crowding the main floor.

But as Zootie climbed up a column, the mezzanine fire doors burst open! Mrs. Hoggett and the landlady stood back-to-back blasting at the pursuing kitchen staff with fire extinguishers.

"Please, try to stay calm," said the grand matriarch over the cries of the crowd around her. Suddenly, Tug jumped up on her lectern.

"Arrgh!" the grand matriarch screamed. "Security! Call security!"

Meanwhile, up on the mezzanine, Mrs. Hoggett turned to the landlady. "Are you with me on this?" she called over the roar of her fire extinguisher.

"All the way, Esme!" the landlady replied.

Mrs. Hoggett continued to hold off the kitchen staff while the landlady raced downstairs to the dance floor. Then the farmer's wife made her way to the edge of the balcony.

"Come, Pig!" she called. "COME, PIG!"

Babe and Ferdinand emerged from between two frothy ball gowns and looked up to see the source of the voice. Thelonius also stared up at the brightly clad figure.

"It looks like Himself," he said.

Easy shook his head. "Thelonius, it isn't."

Whoever it was, the clown was in trouble! Mrs. Hoggett had waiters behind her, guests in front of her, and crazed kitchen staffers in between. There was only one way out!

She climbed up onto the balcony railing, grabbed one of the golden sashes hanging from the room's big crystal chandelier, and jumped!

One waiter reached out to catch her but only caught a corner of a trick handkerchief. It streamed out of her back pocket like a long multi-colored tail.

Babe watched as the farmer's wife swung across the room and landed on the balcony on the other side. "Ferdie," he said to the duck, "things are looking up!"

But the duck was not so sure. "Don't cross your bridges before they hatch," he said.

And the duck was right! Before Babe knew what had happened, he'd been scooped up by the furious chef!

Just then, the landlady emerged from the crowd. "That your pig?" she demanded. "I don't think so!"

She tried to take Babe from the chef while Ferdinand pecked at his feet. But suddenly, waiters grabbed the landlady from behind!

The crowd's cheer was cut short by a cry from above. Mrs. Hoggett had tied the golden sash to her trick suspenders. She looked out over the crowd and shouted, "I AM ESME CORDELIA HOGGETT! AND I'VE COME FOR MY ARTHUR'S PIG!"

With all eyes upon her, Mrs. Hoggett launched

off the balcony and bungee-jumped straight for
Babe!

Unfortunately, Mrs. Hoggett had never bungee-
jumped before. She missed, bouncing back up to the
balcony with only the chef's hat. The chef turned
and made for the kitchen doors, Babe still in his
arms.

Mrs. Hoggett soared once more across the wide
ballroom. Bouncing from table to table like a
weightless astronaut, she finally landed on a food
trolley. She rolled the metal surfboard across the
room right into the chef.

The chef hurtled through the air into a crowded
table. Babe was thrown free! He landed in a mountain of creamy cakes.

"Come, Pig!" Mrs. Hoggett called as she
bounced around the ballroom. "Come, Pig!"

Smeared with pudding and a bit disoriented,
Babe staggered away from the dessert table.

"Incoming! Incoming!" Ferdinand squawked.

Babe looked up just in time to avoid the chef,
who was charging across the dance floor. The crazed
chef jumped up on a table and grabbed Mrs.
Hoggett's legs!

Above them, the huge chandelier creaked omi-
nously. It had not been built to support a bouncing
clown or a mad chef. And at the moment, it was also
sheltering Bob, Zootie, and the twins. Small frag-

ments of plaster drifted down on their heads as they
held on tight.

Below them, the chef clung to Mrs. Hoggett's
shoes. Her trick stockings stretched and stretched
until her legs looked ten feet long! Then the chef
started to whirl her around by her stockings, faster
and faster!

"We have to stop him, Ferdie!" Babe exclaimed.

The pig charged across the dance floor, straight
into the chef's knees. The chef fell backward, yank-
ing the stockings right off of Mrs. Hoggett!

The farmer's wife went flying toward the pyramid of champagne glasses, still guarded by the very
nervous waiter. As his ladder wobbled, he ducked in
time to avoid being smashed by Mrs. Hoggett. But
the waiter recovered his balance in time for Mrs.
Hoggett's return swing…

OOOF! The farmer's wife smashed right into
him. The waiter toppled off his ladder and fell into a
mountain of food. As he scrambled to his feet, he
found a piece of the clown suit in his hand, a big yel-
low tag that said DO NOT PULL.

The waiter looked up to see the farmer's wife
inflating like a giant balloon! As Mrs. Hoggett
bounced around the room, Babe chased after her.
But before he could reach her, three security guards
burst through the main doors. Mrs. Hoggett
watched as a couple of waiters herded the pig toward

the security guards. He was surrounded!

As Mrs. Hoggett prepared to swing to the rescue, the chef climbed up to the opposite balcony and grabbed his own golden sash. He was ready to intercept her!

The farmer's wife jumped.

The chef jumped...and slammed into her! Mrs. Hoggett bounced out of control, barely reaching the opposite balcony.

Suddenly, Thelonius swung into action. The orangutan climbed up to the nearest balcony, grabbed a sash, and swung across the room to land right next to Mrs. Hoggett.

The farmer's wife looked up at the strange creature. Thelonius stared back. Finally, Mrs. Hoggett managed a shy smile.

Then she heard a squeal. The security guards had caught Babe! The pig was being carried, wiggling and squealing, toward an exit. The landlady and the rest of the animals were blocking the way, but how long could they hold out?

And now the chef had been joined on the opposite balcony by a waiter and a guest, each holding a golden sash and ready to jump.

Mrs. Hoggett let out a wild yell and started her swing. But at the last moment, Thelonius reached out and grabbed her, holding her back. It was too late for the three men; they were already swinging

across the room. They swooped ahead of Mrs.
Hoggett and Thelonius, giving the two a clear shot
at Babe.

The security guard carrying the pig looked up in
time to see Esme Cordelia Hoggett descending upon
him like a force of nature. The farmer's wife grabbed
Babe and soared away as the chef, waiter, and guest
collided with each other and plummeted to the
ground.

The farmer's wife and the farmer's pig had been
reunited at last! The two did a victory lap around the
room, followed by a swinging orangutan and a flying
duck. The landlady and the other animals beamed
with pride. Even the guests cheered.

If only the weight of the orangutan, the pig, and
the farmer's wife had not finally overloaded the chandelier. With a crunch, it ripped from its moorings.

Bob and Zootie gave a cry and quickly jumped to
a nearby net holding thousands of balloons. The net
released and the chimps rode it to safety. Mrs.
Hoggett and Babe bounced clear as the chandelier
crashed to the ground.

In the shocked moment of silence that followed,
thousands of balloons gently floated down. Slowly,
the guests began emerging from under tables. Faces
usually frowning at board meetings were alive with
smiles.

Onstage, Tug began playing with the balloons,

batting them this way and that. Across the room, the pink poodle found the handsome bull terrier lying on the ground. She licked his ear.

"Oh, big guy, are you okay?" she asked.

The bull terrier thought he was dreaming: that soft voice, that pink fur!

He opened his eyes. "I am now...my little fumphful."

But misery is often the neighbor of happiness. A few feet away, Zootie searched through the debris of the broken chandelier. She was frantic.

"One of the babies is missing!" she said.

Babe looked up at the tall ceiling. High above, in the hole where the chandelier used to be, the pig saw something move. He squinted his eyes. Babe could just make out a tiny ball of dark fur. The baby chimp was clinging to a fragment of plaster!

Suddenly, the little fellow sneezed, and the plaster started to crumble.

"Thelonius!" Babe shouted.

Across the room, directly under the little chimp, the orangutan was helping Mrs. Hoggett to her feet.

Babe ran over to them. *"Thelonius!"*

The orangutan turned to the pig just as Babe cried, "Look!"

With one final tiny sneeze, the plaster broke! The baby plummeted toward the ground. Somewhere, a woman screamed.

"What?" Thelonius said.

"Look up!" Babe shouted.

Thelonius looked up at the ceiling and, at the last moment, thrust out his arms.

PLOP!

The tiny chimp landed safely in Thelonius's hands.

Up on stage, the grand matriarch let out a little sigh. "Much more exciting than last year," she said. Her twinkling, beady eyes looked very much like a pig's...

Zootie looked up from the tiny twins resting in her arms. "Thank you," she told Thelonius.

"Yeah, Thelonius. Thank you," Bob added.

Thelonius stared at Bob, then said, "Thank the pig."

The Flealands Hotel would never be the same. Colored lights pulsed in time to the music pouring from its freshly painted windows. A bold neon sign read: DANCELANDS.

The neighbors across the canal turned up their opera, but they couldn't drown out the noise.

"We were better off with the animals, Hortense," said the man.

His wife nodded glumly. She was more miserable than ever.

But not every change is for the worse. Sometimes

a good thing is cut down, but grows back even stronger, or two broken halves make something new, something more complete.

At least that's what the farmer's wife and the landlady had decided. And so it was that the hotel was rented out, thus providing the wherewithal for a curious arrangement.

The one-time residents of the Flealands Hotel and nearby Cardboard City soon found themselves breathing fresh country air. They all relocated to Hoggett Hollow. The landlady took to riding her bike along the country road leading to Hoggett's farm. Nigel and Alan liked to trot along behind her.

Flealick found the pace of country life too slow. Recalling his wild ride clinging to the hospital van, the little dog took to chasing trucks. Hanging on the mud flap of a roaring delivery van made Flealick's morning.

Inspired by their new, natural setting, the chimpanzees decided to be chimpanzees. Bob, Zootie, Easy, and the little twins took up residence in an idyllic patch of rainforest near the farm.

As for the orangutan, he insisted on staying at the farmhouse with Herself. Thelonius watched Mrs. Hoggett's every move as she hung up laundry on the line.

Mrs. Hoggett took a while to adjust to the orangutan's adoring presence.

"Shoo, shoo," the farmer's wife said. But she had found a friend for life.

Sad to say, the thing between the bull terrier and the pink poodle didn't last. The poodle ran off with another dog and left him with the kids.

"Ya gotta be scary," the bull terrier urged his pink-haired offspring. "You're warriors! Now let's hear that snarl!"

The little bull poodles whined, "But, Daaad. Do we have to?"

And finally, dear ones, the pig and the farmer were content again in each other's company. And things were back to where they had started…more or less.

Farmer Hoggett turned the spigot. Deep down in the well, the new pump rumbled to life. Farmer and pig watched the tap. A gurgle, then a splutter, then a gush of clear water spurted from the shiny spout!

The farmer turned to his pig. "That'll do, Pig," he said. "That'll do."